NOTHING WILL EVER BE THE SAME.

Riley picked his nose.

10:15.

Strawberries.

The proton is dead.

These things will go together forever.

My dad remembers exactly what he was doing the moment he heard that Elvis died. For my mother, it was Princess Di. It will be that way with me and the proton.

OTHER BOOKS BY JERRY SPINELLI

Maniac Magee

Wringer

Loser

Space Station Seventh Grade

Jason and Marceline

Who Put That Hair in My Toothbrush?

There's a Girl in My Hammerlock

Crash

The Library Card

Stargirl

Milkweed

Eggs

Love, Stargirl

JERRY SPINELLI

Smiles to Go

JOANNA COTLER BOOKS

HARPER

An Imprint of HarperCollins*Publishers*

Smiles to Go

Copyright © 2008 by Jerry Spinelli

Library of Congress Cataloging-in-Publication Data
Spinelli, Jerry.
    Smiles to go / Jerry Spinelli. — 1st ed.
      p. cm.
    Summary: Will Tuppence's life has always been ruled by science and
common sense, but in ninth grade, shaken up by the discovery that protons decay, he begins to see the entire world differently and gains new
perspective on his relationships with his little sister and two close friends.
    ISBN 978-0-06-447197-8
    [1. Brothers and sisters—Fiction. 2. Friendship—Fiction. 3. Self-
actualization (Psychology)—Fiction. 4. Family life—Fiction. 5. High
schools—Fiction. 6. Schools—Fiction.] I. Title.
PZ7.S75663Smi 2008   2007029563
[Fic]—dc22   CIP
                                             AC

Typography by Carla Weise
09 10 11 12 13   CG/CW   10 9 8 7 6 5 4 3 2 1
❖
First paperback edition, 2009

ACKNOWLEDGMENTS

My gratitude to the following, in chronological order of their contributions: Sean James, Lois Ferguson, Ginee Seo, Ben Spinelli, Alyson McDonough, Ryan James, Will Merola, Linda Sue Park, Rod Adams, Dan Heisman, Ashley Merola, and Andrew Rosencrans. With double thanks to my editor, Joanna Cotler, my cousin Dr. Patty Maud, and my wife and favorite author, Eileen.

To my schoolmates
Norristown High School
Class of '59

UNSMASHABLE

When I was five or six a high-school kid lived next door. His name was Jim. He was a science nut. He won the county science fair two years in a row and went on to MIT. I think he works for NASA now.

Jim was always tinkering in his basement. I was welcome, encouraged even, to join him whenever I liked. I would sit on a high stool for hours and just watch him. I think he enjoyed having a dedicated audience of one.

Jim built his own shortwave radio that we both listened to. He practically swooned when he heard scratchy voices from the South Pacific, but I was too young to be amazed. He always had a jawbreaker in his mouth, and when he wasn't clacking it against his teeth he kept up a constant mutter about everything he did, as if he were a play-by-play announcer describing a game. "And now Jim is soldering the wire to the whatsits. . . ."

More than anything I looked forward to Jim saying, "Whoa!" That's what he said when something surprised or astounded him. It didn't happen often, maybe only one or two "Whoas!" a week on average. When I heard one I would jump down from my stool and nose right in and say, "What, Jim?" And he would explain it to me, and though I couldn't really understand, still I would feel something, a cool fizzing behind my ears, because I was feeding off his astonishment.

Then one day I had the real thing, an amazement of my own. That day was a little strange to begin with, because when I came down to the basement, Jim wasn't tinkering— he was reading. Watching a person read isn't the most fascinating thing in the world, even if he has a jawbreaker clacking around in his mouth, and after a minute of that I was ready to leave when Jim barked out a "Whoa!" I jumped down and said my usual, "What, Jim?" but he only warded me off with his hand and kept on reading. Every minute or so another "Whoa!" came out, each one louder than the last. Then came three in a row: "Whoa! Whoa! WWWHOA!"

"Jim! *What*!" I screeched and snatched the book away.

He looked at me as if he didn't know me. Young as I was, I understood that he was still back in the book, immersed in his amazement.

Finally he said it, one word: "Protons." I had heard people say "amen" in that tone of voice.

"What are protons?" I said.

He took the book from my hands. His eyes returned to the present. He began talking, explaining. He talked about atoms first, the tiny building blocks of everything, smaller than molecules, smaller than specks. "So small," he said, "millions can fit in a flea's eye." That got my attention.

One of the most amazing things about atoms, he said, is that, tiny as they are, they are mostly empty space. That made no sense to me. Empty space was nothing. How could a "something" be nothing? He knocked on his stool seat. "Empty space." I knocked the stool seat. Empty space? Then why did it stop my hand?

He said atoms are kind of like miniature solar systems. Instead of planets circling the sun, electrons circle a nugget of protons. Then he zeroed in on protons. Atoms may be mostly space, he said, but a proton is nothing but a proton. Small as an atom is, a proton is millions of times smaller. "You could squint till your eyeballs pop out and you'll never see one," he said, daring me to try.

"And you know what the coolest thing about protons is?" he said.

"What?" I said.

He clacked his jawbreaker for a while, building the suspense. "You can't do anything to them," he said. "You can't break them. You can't burn them. You can't blow them up. Atoms you can smash, but you can't smash a proton."

"Not even with a *steamroller*?" I said.

"Not even with a thousand steamrollers."

And then he hammered home his point. He took out the jawbreaker and put it on the floor. He took a hammer and smashed it to smithereens. He didn't stop there. He kept smashing until there was nothing but white powder. When he stopped, he grinned at me. "Go ahead, stomp on it." I brought the heel of my shoe down on the tiny pile of powder. "Oh, come on, don't be such a wuss," he said. "Stomp good." I did. I jumped up and down until there was nothing on the floor but a pale mist of dust. He got down on his hands and knees and blew it away.

I cheered. "We did it!"

He stood. "What did we do?" he said.

"We smashed the jawbreaker. We made it disappear."

"We sure did," he said. "But what about the protons that made up the jawbreaker? Where are they?"

I looked around. "Gone?"

He shook his head with a sly smile. "Nope," he said. "The jawbreaker is gone, but not its protons. They're still"—he waved his hand about the basement—"here. They'll always be here. They're unsmashable. Once a proton, always a proton. Protons are forever."

The next words just popped from my mouth, no real thought behind them: "Jawbreakers are lucky."

He poked me. "Hey, so are you. You're made of protons, too."

I stared at him. "I *am*?"

"Sure," he said. "Zillions of them. The protons in you are the same as the protons in that jawbreaker. And in that stool. And in a banana. And a sock monkey. And a glass of water. And a star. Everything"—he threw out his arms—"everything is made of protons!"

I was getting woozy with information overload. Me and sock monkeys made of the same stuff? It was too much to digest. So I retreated to the one conclusion I had managed to extract from all this. "So . . . Jim . . . like, I'm unsmashable?"

He mussed my hair. "Yeah," he said, "I guess you could sort of put it that way." He laughed and waved the hammer in my face. "But don't go trying this on your toe."

Riley picked his nose.

10:15.

Strawberries.

The proton is dead.

These things will go together forever.

My dad remembers exactly what he was doing the moment he heard that Elvis died. For my mother, it was Princess Di. It will be that way with me and the proton.

I was at the kitchen counter this morning cutting strawberries in half, dropping the pieces into my bowl of bite-size Mini-Wheats. My little sister, Tabby, came into the kitchen saying, "Riley picked his nose . . . Riley picked his nose. . . ." She's learning to read, and whenever she sees a few words that strike her fancy she keeps repeating them with a snooty I-can-read smirk.

So Tabby said, "Riley picked his nose," and the knife sliced open the smell of strawberries and the phone on the wall rang. Tabby got to it first. She always does. "Barney's Saloon." That's how she answers the phone these days. She listened for a moment and said into the mouthpiece: "Phooey!" This is what she says whenever a caller asks for anyone but her. She jabbed the phone in my face. "For *yyew*."

It was Mi-Su's voice. Excited. "Ninety-eight point five FM! Quick!"

Click.

I ran for the radio, snapped it on . . . FM . . . 98.5. Saturday morning news-of-the-week roundup. Man's voice:

" . . . years of waiting. Finally it happened. The telltale flash that signaled the death of the proton, the moment when it ceased to be. Scientists around the world are speculating on the significance . . ."

I couldn't believe it. A proton was dead! Caught in the act of dying. One moment it was there, then it wasn't.

I looked at the clock. 10:15. Saturday. September 26. And, for me, the start of a new calendar: PD1 (The Day I Heard of the Proton's Death).

Tabby was standing on a chair at the counter. She was slicing a sweet potato.

"Don't," I told her. She stuck out her tongue at me.

The phone rang. This time I got it.

"Hear it?" Mi-Su.

"Yeah."

"So what do you think?" Her voice was bouncy.

Tabby was dropping two slices of sweet potato into the toaster. "Don't!" I said.

"Don't what?" said Mi-Su.

"I'm talking to Tabby. I can't believe it."

"Why not?"

"All those years, nothing happened. Now . . ."

"Proton de-*cay-ay*." She sang it.

"Why are you so happy?"

"I'm excited, that's all. It's news. A discovery. Nothing will ever be the same."

"That's good?" I said.

"Who knows? It just is. Proton decay. It's a fact of life."

The toaster popped. Tabby pulled out the two slices of sweet potato toast and laid them in a cereal bowl. She climbed up onto the counter, both feet, stood there daring me to do something about it. She got the peanut butter, scooped out a glob with her finger and spread it over the slices. She got the brown sugar. She grabbed a chunk, crumbled it over the peanut butter. She stood on the edge of the counter. She gave me her snooty smirk, spoke.

"Riley—"

"Don't," I said.

"Picked—"

"Don't."

"His—"

"I'm telling you!"

"Nose!"

She jumped from the counter to the floor. Dishes rattled. She grabbed her potato toast and raced upstairs to her Saturday morning cartoons.

"Will? You there?"

"Yeah."

"What was that noise?"

"My sister. Jumping down from the kitchen counter."

"She's too much."

"She just did nineteen things she's not supposed to do."

"To bug you, that's why."

"That's what my mother says."

"You're lucky. I wish I had a little sister."

"Take this one."

She laughed. "We playing tonight?"

"I guess."

"My house, right?"

"Yeah."

"So you bring."

We play Monopoly on Saturday nights. One person hosts the game, the other brings the pizza. Three mediums. BT comes, but he doesn't buy, he just plays. He's always broke.

"The usual?" I said.

"*Extra* pepperoni," she said. "And don't let your stinky pizza get anywhere *near* me. Last time, some of your anchovy fumes crawled over my cheese. I could taste them."

"*I* can taste the fumes from your pepperoni breath. Excuse me—*extra* pepperoni breath."

She always gets extra pepperoni. I always get anchovies and extra sauce. We always fight about it.

"You're a sicko," she said. "Why can't you just get pepperoni or extra cheese like the rest of the world? Nobody gets extra *sauce*."

"I do."

"Because you're not normal. Bye."

"Wait!"

"What?"

"I just heard the tail end of it on the radio," I said. "Where did it happen?"

"Yellowknife. They charge me for your extras, you know."

"Sue me. Bye."

"Bye."

As soon as I hung up, the phone rang again.

She was giggling. "Sue me. That's my name backwards. Bye." *Click.*

I went back to my strawberries. When I had them all in halves, I started cutting them into quarters. I looked at my reflection in the toaster. I looked pinched. Loopy.

A fact of life.

I poured Mini-Wheats into the bowl. Added the strawberries. Got a spoon. Sat at the table. Poured milk. Not too much. I don't like soggy cereal. . . .

The clock said 10:28.

Thirteen minutes and counting.

Nothing will ever be the same.

I stared into the strawberries. Except for the cartoon noise upstairs, the house was silent. Dad was golfing. Mom was at the Arts Center, taking watercolor lessons.

Now pounding from upstairs. Tabby was hammering something. She has her own plastic tools, but she uses most of them to eat with. For serious vandalism she prefers my father's real tools, which she's been forbidden to touch since she nailed his slipper to the floor. She steals them when it's just the two of us in the house. She knows she can hammer away and I won't stop her as long as she's not in my room.

My spoon broke through strawberries, sank into cereal.

The proton was dead.

Riley picked his nose.

■ ■ ■

Colossal tanks holding thousands of gallons of water sit at the bottom of salt mines and coal mines around the world. Japan. South Africa. Europe. Canada. Supersensitive instruments monitor the water. Trillions of molecules of water—every one watched 24/7/365. For years. Decades.

The instruments have been waiting for a flash. The tiniest, most invisible of all flashes. A flash that would mean that a proton—one of the gazillion protons making up the trillions of water molecules—had suddenly winked out of existence. The flash would prove proton decay really happens. The flash would mean that the matter of the proton—the solid stuff— had turned into the energy of the flash ($E=mc^2$). Totally. Nothing left behind. No ash. No smoke. No smell. Nada. One moment it's there, the next moment—pffft—gone.

What would it mean? Only this: Nothing lasts. Nothing. Because everything that exists is made of protons.

Decades went by. No flashes. Untold gazillions of protons under watch, and not a single flash. It looked like the universe would last forever.

And then it happened. It happened in the tank two miles below the earth in Yellowknife, Northwest Territories, Canada, Middle of

Nowhere. It happened in the thirty-third year of watching. Eight days ago, says the Centauri Dreams website. Friday night. At precisely 9:47:55 eastern standard time. They saw it. They recorded it. A flash.

— — —

The money was stacked. The cards were stacked. We were both on our second slice. Waiting for BT. Anthony Bontempo.

"Pizza's getting cold," I said. "Let's just start. Teach him a lesson for once." I rolled the dice.

Mi-Su snatched them up. "No! He'll be here."

"He knows we start at seven. Let's show him we can play without him. Then maybe he'll learn to be on time."

She gave me rolling eyes. "Yeah, right. He's BT, remember?"

She was right. BT will be late for his own funeral.

Commotion upstairs. Mi-Su's parents squealing: "BT!" The dog squealing. The dog doesn't squeal like that when I come over.

BT clumped down the stairs. "Gimme four hotels on Park Place!" He rolled his skateboard into the corner. It bumped into mine. BT snatched one of Mi-Su's slices. Mi-Su screamed, threw a pillow at him.

"Clowns," I said. "I'm going first." We sprawled over the floor. I rolled the dice.

BT's first roll was a three. Baltic Avenue. He bought it for $60. He fished in his pile for the money. Mi-Su and I keep our money in stacks of ones, fives, etc. BT always buys the first thing he lands on. And I always have to say something.

"Dumb."

He said what he always says: "I'm wheelin' and dealin'."

"If I land there," I told him, "all you'll get out of me is four dollars rent. The most you'll ever get with a hotel there is four hundred and fifty."

"Wheelin' and dealin'," he said. He went to the fridge for a soda.

After three times around the board, BT had bought everything he landed on: Baltic, Mediterranean, Vermont, Electric Company,

Tennessee, Kentucky, Water Works, Marvin Gardens, Short Line, Boardwalk. Of course he was broke now, but he didn't care. "Wheelin' and dealin'!" Monopoly money or real money—heck, life itself—it all comes down to one word for BT: spend. I don't think he can even spell the word "save."

BT's strategy (I'm being funny using that word in the same sentence as BT) for Monopoly has two parts:

1. Buy everything you land on until you run out of money.
2. Love the railroads.

He actually believes that if he can ever land on all four railroads and buy them, that's the day he'll win.

Busted, BT was ripe for a buyout. I couldn't stand seeing Boardwalk, the most valuable property of all, in his hands. I offered him what he paid for it—$400. He took it. Mi-Su shrieked in pain.

Pretty soon I landed on Park Place, too, so I could build on the blue. Mi-Su got the green. As usual, it came down to me and her.

"Hear the news?" I said to BT.

He looked at me, shocked. "I didn't know anybody knew," he said.

I looked at Mi-Su, back at BT. "What are you talking about?"

"I went down Dead Man's Hill."

"Wow!" gushed Mi-Su. "When?"

"Last night."

"Skateboard?"

BT took a swig of soda. "All the way."

"And you're *alive*?"

He pinched himself. "I ain't dead."

"I'm talking about the proton," I said.

BT frowned. "What proton?"

"The one that died. It finally happened. Now there's proof."

"Yeah?" He tried to steal one of Mi-Su's pepperonis. She grabbed his wrist and bit his hand till he let go.

"You want to hear about it?" I said.

"Sure," he said. He snarled at Mi-Su. "Carnivore."

I told him what happened at Yellowknife. As I was talking, he rolled the dice. He landed on Community Chest. He picked up the top card. He looked at it. A huge grin crossed his face.

"Are you listening?" I said.

Now his face was smug. Proud. Superior. He read from the card: "Collect fifty dollars from every player."

Mi-Su tossed him a fifty.

"Do you know what this means?" I said.

"Yeah"—he waggled his fingers in my face—"fifty big ones, chump."

"It means matter is mortal. Everything is going to go. Disappear. Vanish. Rock. Water. The planets. The stars. *Everything.*"

He blinked. "Pepperonis, too?"

Mi-Su howled.

"Cretin," I said.

"So, when's all this going to happen?"

"Way in the future," I said. "Billions of years."

He looked at me, the smirk gone. "*Billions* of years?"

"Trillions, actually."

He cocked his head, stared at me, honestly puzzled. He turned to Mi-Su. She nodded. He swung back to me. The smirk returned. The waggling fingers were back in my face. "Fifty."

I crumpled up a fifty and threw it at him.

"He doesn't care about anything," I said to Mi-Su.

Mi-Su grinned. "He's a mess."

We do this, talk about BT as if he's not there.

"That's the word. He's the most messy, disorganized person I know. He has no—"

"—discipline." Mi-Su rolled the dice. She landed on green. Pacific Avenue. "I'm building."

"Right. Discipline. Absolutely none. He just flops and slops through life."

Mi-Su laughed. "A floppy slopper!"

BT laughed. "A sloppy flopper!"

Sometimes he joins in, talking about himself as if he's not there.

Mi-Su built four houses on Pacific Avenue.

"He has no sense of time," I said. "He does everything zippo—like that"—I snapped my fingers—"spur of the moment. No thought. Spends money the instant he gets it."

"He doesn't need pockets."

"He doesn't think. He just does." I rolled the dice.

"A nonthinking doer."

I landed on Park Place. "He spends all his money buying cheap stuff that he can never win with."

"Railroads!"

"Exactly."

"He's disgraceful."

"Perverted," said BT.

"But he thinks he can do it." I built a hotel on Park Place. "And look what he's using. The *thimble*. He's a *boy*."

"Don't be sexist."

Unlike the rest of the world, BT doesn't have a favorite Monopoly token. (I always use the top hat; Mi-Su always uses the dog.) He never chooses his token. He just blindly snatches one up.

"I'm just trying to set him straight," I said. "Be a good role model."

Mi-Su pointed at me. "He skateboarded down Dead Man's Hill."

"So he says."

BT rolled the dice.

Mi-Su looked at me, wide-eyed. "You don't believe him?"

No one has ever skateboarded down Dead

Man's Hill. It comes down off Heather Lane. It's unpaved, stony, rutted, twisting and so steep that when you stand at the top, the faraway bottom almost meets the tip of your board.

BT landed on Park Place.

"He'd be dead," I said. "Rent fifteen hundred."

"I believe him," said Mi-Su.

Deep down, I believed him, too, but I didn't want to. I waggled my fingers in his face. "Fifteen hundred."

It was comical, BT picking through his couple of tens and twenties, as if fifteen hundred dollars was going to appear out of nowhere.

Mi-Su sent a whisper: "Mortgage."

BT threw a finger in the air. "I'll mortgage!" He mortgaged all his properties (except of course Short Line Railroad). "Wheelin' and dealin'."

He dumped all his money in front of me. I counted it. "You're six hundred and eighty short."

"I did something else, too," he said.

Wide-eyed, Mi-Su, who always bites: "What?"

BT shook his head. "Not telling."

I waggled. "Six hundred and eighty, please."

"BT—*what*?" Mi-Su whined. "Tell me."

BT shook his head no.

"Tell me and I'll give you a loan." She counted it out. "Six hundred and eighty."

"Oh, no," I said. I waved the rule book at her. I read: "'Money can be loaned to a player only by the Bank.'"

Mi-Su snooted. "It's my money. I can do whatever I want." She waved the money under BT's nose. "Tell."

BT snatched the money, leaned across the board and whispered in her ear. Her eyes bulged. She squealed, "Really?"

He put on a fake shy face, closed his eyes, nodded. He plunked the money down in front of me. "Rent paid."

Not that it did him much good. Twice more around the board and he landed on Boardwalk, where I also had a hotel. Rent $2,000. He was dead. "I lose," he said brightly. He tossed his thimble in the box and headed for the dartboard.

There's no satisfaction in beating BT, because he doesn't even care if he loses. He cheats you that way.

As usual, Mi-Su and I went on with the game, but something was different. The squares on the board seemed to float under my little silver top hat. BT had done Dead Man's Hill, and Mi-Su knew something I didn't, and the proton was dead.

PD3

Monday morning.

The principal finished talking over the PA, and the student announcer for the day took over. She talked about how to nominate people for Wildcat and Wildkitten of the Month, then she said, "And on Friday night, Anthony Bontempo, Homeroom two thirteen, became the first person ever to skateboard down Dead Man's Hill!"

Cheers erupted from forty homerooms.

Morning announcements ended with no

mention of the proton.

In the hallways the mobs heading for classes were buzzing:

"BT!"

"He's crazy!"

"Insane!"

"I knew he'd be the one!"

Funny thing, nobody questioned whether it was true or not. Nobody said maybe BT made the whole thing up. Everybody knows BT doesn't lie. If you don't care about consequences, about anything, you don't have to lie. And it's not like he did Dead Man's Hill for the glory. If that were true, he would have had witnesses. He just did it for the same reason he does everything else—he felt like it.

— — —

Third period. Physics. Mr. Sigfried.

Finally, somebody to share the proton news with.

The teacher leaned back against the desk, arms folded. "OK, people—there was big news over the weekend. Something happened that will cause textbooks to be rewritten. Who would like to tell us what I'm referring to?"

My hand was already up when Jamie Westphal blurted, "Anthony Bontempo skateboarded down Dead Man's Hill!"

Hoots, whistles, cheers, standing ovation—and BT wasn't even in the class. Even Mr. Sigfried gave him a little pitty clap. Then he called on me.

I waited for total silence and said, "Proton decay. It's confirmed."

He snapped a finger at me. "Give that man a prize. And what exactly does that mean, Mr. Tuppence? Proton decay."

"It means nothing in the universe will last."

He went into mock shock. "Nothing?"

"Nothing."

"How so, Mr. Tuppence?"

"Because everything is made of protons. And now we know that even protons don't last forever. Therefore everything will disappear."

"The planets, too? They're going to disappear?"

"Yep."

"The stars?"

"Yep."

26

"My aunt Tilly's teapot?"

"Yep." I was enjoying this.

He gazed out the window. "And when is this great disappearing going to happen, Mr. Tuppence?"

"Long time from now."

"Long time? Like a year from now?"

I snickered. "Way longer."

Jamie Westphal piped up, "So, how long?"

Mr. Sigfried gave me a palms-up stop sign. "Let me answer that one, Mr. Tuppence. It's kinda fun." He turned to the blackboard and chalked a 1 in the upper-left corner and began writing zeroes and commas across the whole board. And across the board again. And again. He must have gone on for a full five minutes before he plunked the chalk down, stepped aside and gestured at the board covered with the most colossal number any of us had ever seen. "That"—he grinned—"many years."

"Zowie!" somebody said.

Somebody whistled.

Somebody farted.

The class cracked up. Mr. Sigfried wagged his head and began erasing the board. "OK,

people," he said, "back to earth. Today we con-
sider"—He lettered the rest on the dusty blackboard:

THE WONDERS OF WATER

— — —

After school I drubbed Mi-Su in chess club
and headed home on Black Viper, my skateboard. Bones Swiss bearings gave the wheels a
buttery whir beneath my feet.

I was still a block from my house when I
heard Tabby screaming, "Will, look at me!"

BT has been teaching Tabby to skateboard
lately. She was wobbling down the driveway.
She fell off before she reached the sidewalk.
She jumped up, lugged the board back to the
garage and wobbled down again. She threw
out her arms—"Look!"—and toppled off again.

"No showboating," said BT.

"Will," said Tabby, "can I use Black Viper?"

"No," I told her.

"Pleeeeze!" She carefully laid a sneaker toe
on Black Viper.

I kicked her foot away. I stepped off. I
picked up the board. She was looking straight

up at me. Her eyes seemed to take up half her face. I hated BT for getting her started on this. I said, "Don't ever—*ever*—touch this skateboard. *Ever*. Or you will *die*."

The eyes blinked. She wanted to cry but she wouldn't let herself. For once in her life she was going to obey me.

I shot BT a glare and headed for the front door.

Tabby piped behind me: "BT went down Dead Man's Hill!"

"Big deal," I said, and went inside.

PD7

There I was but I didn't know why.

I had told my parents I had to go to school early to help a teacher. Sunrise was the only time of day I could be sure no other kids would be around. They've been going up there all week—pilgrims on skateboards—just to be near the place, to stand where he stood, to look over the edge of Dead Man's Hill, to feel the tingle on the backs of their necks, to try to picture themselves doing it, to laugh and back off.

So far no one else has done it. Sooner or later somebody will. It won't be me.

The town lay below me. Roofs. Trees. Streets. Sticking up like a periscope: the clock tower on the corner of the Brimley Building. I could see the round face of the clock, but not the time.

The rising sun was straight ahead. I could look directly at it because it was bloody orange and just over the horizon and smoky with clouds. When I looked at the sun, my eyes were crossing 93 million miles of space. But my feet wouldn't cross another inch.

I had one foot on Black Viper, one foot on the earth. There was already too much space under the tip of the board. The angle of the drop was astounding. I felt as if I was looking down over the roof edge of a skyscraper. I didn't see how his wheels could have stayed on the ground all the way down. At some point he must have been flying. And then there were the stones and shin-deep ruts.

I thought: *This is impossible. He lied.*

I knew I was wrong.

Why was I doing this? I knew I wouldn't go down. I was scared stiff just standing there. I already knew I was a coward. Did I need to prove it? Remind myself? Ninety-three million miles of space in front of me, and every inch of it seemed packed with the things I was afraid of: high places, cramped places, dark places, thousand-leggers, speed, flying, death, change, time, pain, failure, criticism, roller coasters, train tracks, being wrong, being smelly, being late, being stupid, being rejected, black mambos, leeches, hantavirus, losing, deep water, uncertainty, being buried alive, being caught being afraid, myself . . .

I could see my epitaph:

HERE LIES WILLIAM JAY TUPPENCE
HE WAS AFRAID

Of course, that wouldn't really happen, because no one knows this about me, not even my parents. What everyone sees is a pretty normal-looking kid, 5 feet 9 $^1/_2$ inches, brown hair, brown eyes, ears a little big, a little stuck out but not enough to mock. Likes science, especially astronomy. Best friends: Anthony Bontempo (aka BT) and Mi-Su Kelly. Runs cross-country. Chess Club. Good at it. Won a trophy. Calls his skateboard Black Viper. Rides it to school. A little shy, on the quiet side, but friendly enough. Not the life of the party, but not a hermit either. Somewhere in the middle. Sensible.

If I'm famous for anything, I guess that's it. I'm sensible. Other kids ask my advice about stuff. To me common sense is just that: common. But some kids seem to think it's this rare gift. They seem to see me as a substitute adult. A homeroom kid wrote in my eighth-grade yearbook: "Thank you for your wisdom & wise ways." Doug Lawson, a cross-country running mate, calls me "Old Man."

That's the macro view. Down here on quantum level, where I live by myself, my fears quiver like leaping electrons. I send my questions up to the surface, but they fizzle long before they reach the top. Why can't I be like other kids? Why can't I believe I'm indestructible? Why can't I believe I'll live forever?

Why do I stare at the sky at night?

Suddenly the sun was blinding. I panicked. Had I gone too far? The clock tower wobbled. I kicked Black Viper back. I stepped away from the terrifying drop. I climbed on my board and pushed off, back to where I belonged, my wheels whirring over the asphalt.

PD8

Saturday morning. Downtown. Hicks' Sporting Goods.

Mr. Hicks handed me the trophy. This was my father's idea. When I won the chess tournament last spring, my father looked at the inscription—

HOPE COUNTY
CHESS CHAMPION
AGES 13–15

—and said, "They should have put your name on it."

"How could they?" I said. "They didn't know I was going to win."

"I knew," he said.

So typical. My father has so much confidence in me, it's scary. They say that when I was a baby, one year old, he tossed me into the deep end of the Crescent Club pool (my mother screaming), and I swam.

It's been kind of like that ever since. He knows what I can do before I know. In fifth grade he told me I would be the school spelling champion, and I was. He said I would learn to ride a bicycle in one hour. I did. I wish I could be as fearless for myself as he is for me.

"Here ya go," said Mr. Hicks.

I looked at the inscription, added at the bottom of the black mirror plate:

WILL TUPPENCE

"Congratulations," he said. "I never got the hang of chess myself." He chuckled. "Checkers for me." He was still holding it.

The trophy was beautiful. It was topped by a pewter King Arthur–looking figure standing on a board of little black-and-white squares. The five-inch base was blue marbled stone and held the inscription plate. I already had a space for it on the bookcase in my room.

Finally he let go. "It's figuring out all those moves ahead of time," he said. "I don't know how you do it. I hear the real experts—"

"Grand masters."

"Yeah, the grand masters, they know what they're gonna do—what, three moves ahead?"

"Try ten," I said.

His eyes boggled. He whistled.

"Well, thanks again," I said.

I headed home on foot. I wasn't taking a chance on crashing Black Viper with priceless freight on board. I walked past the old Brimley Building clock tower. It said 11:45. My watch said 11:55. The clock tower is famous for being right. I reset my watch. Hopefully, in a couple of months, I won't have this problem. I've told my parents I want a radio-controlled Exacta watch for Christmas. I showed them the ad in *Discover*. Every night it receives a signal from the National Institute of Standards and Technology Atomic Clock in

Fort Collins, Colorado. The Atomic Clock is accurate to within ten billionths of a second (0.000000001 sec).

For some reason I looked back at the clock tower. It's one of those old-fashioned clocks, with Roman numerals instead of Arabic numbers. Suddenly on the right shoulder of the ten (X), I saw a tiny flash, like a glint from the sun. But when I looked up at the sky, it was gray, nothing but clouds.

— — —

Tonight Monopoly will be at my house. Mi-Su will bring the pizza, anchovies and extra sauce for me, extra pepperoni for her. And a small regular for Tabby. I'll tell her not to do that, that Tabby is just a little kid, that she already thinks she's a grown-up and treating her like one of us will just make her worse. She'll ignore me and give my sister the pizza. BT will be late. Tabby will race upstairs, go crazy over him. He'll breeze down to the basement den and call ahead: "Gimme four hotels on Park Place!" He'll buy everything he lands on. He'll chuckle when he gets a railroad.

Tabby will cheer him on. Within an hour he'll be wiped out. Tabby will attack him. They'll wrestle. She'll bring him a book, probably an adult murder mystery. He'll spend the rest of the night reading it to her. He'll leave out the bad words.

PD16

Sunday morning. Church. Boring, as usual. But as my father says, it's money in the bank. It's the ticket. The bridge. It's how to get from Here to There. From Here to Forever.

There's always a pencil in the pew. Stubby, yellow, like the ones they give you at miniature golf to keep score with. As the service dragged on, I checked off the items in the program: Call to Worship, Hymn of Praise, Prayer of Adoration, Prayer of Confession, Assurance of Pardon, etc., etc. Then came the dreaded sermon—talk about Forever! This was the third Sunday since the proton died in Yellowknife, and Rev. Mauger hadn't said a word about it.

Neither has anyone else. The world doesn't seem to care about the end of itself.

The reverend's lullaby droned on. I decided to amuse myself by writing down Mr. Sigfried's number. Across the top of the church program, down the right-hand side, across the bottom and halfway up the left side:

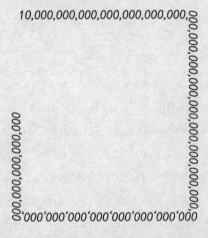

I stared at the number. It made no sense. It's beyond gazillions. There's not even a name for it. It's the number of years from now when everything will be gone. If I could live that long, I would see Rev. Mauger's pulpit evaporate, proton by proton.

The number was making me woozy. So I did what I sometimes do when I feel lost in time and space—I began writing down my famous (to me) twelve-step plan:

1. born
2. grow up
3. school
4. college (Naval Academy)
5. career (astronomer)
6. wife (blonde, named Emily, Jennifer or Ann)
7. kids (2)
8. house (four bathrooms)
9. car (mint condition, black 1985 Jaguar XJS/12)
10. retire (win senior chess tournaments)
11. death
12. Heaven (angel) (Forever)

Except now, considering the news from Yellowknife, there's a parade of question marks after number 12. Like, are angels made of protons? Is Heaven? If so, does this mean they won't last forever?

And what exactly is Heaven anyway? A thing? A place? I don't think so. I mean, if I could look at a map of creation, there wouldn't be a sign saying, "Heaven—This Way." My opinion? Heaven is a dimension, like time. Like up and down.

I think.

As for angels, what are they made of? Smoke? Vapor? Holograms? No. Angels are spirits, and a spirit—by definition—is non-stuff.

I think.

I hope.

I turned the church program over and stared again at the unbelievable number. And risked the biggest question of all: When all this time, all these numbers go by, when the last iota of stuff in the universe—the last proton— finally winks out, will Forever still be? Does Forever continue on beyond the last zero? My answer (my prayer?): of course it does, because Forever means endless.

So . . .

If Heaven and angels are non-stuff . . .

If the stuff-me becomes after death a non-stuff angel-me . . .

If Heaven and angels exist in a timeless medium we call Forever ("Hey, nobody here but us angels!") . . .

Then . . . guess what? . . .

There will be no end of me!
Will Tuppence Forever!

If.

Suddenly we were on our feet singing the last hymn. On the drive home I discovered the little yellow pencil was still in my hand.

PD19

English. The only class I share with BT. Mrs. Hartenstine, the teacher, is old-fashioned. She believes in memorizing. She says, "Memorized passages should be a part of every person's wardrobe, like shirts and shoes."

Today we recited the poems she assigned us to learn. My poem was "The End of the World" by Archibald MacLeish. Mi-Su did "I'm Nobody! Who Are You?" by Emily Dickinson.

When Mrs. Hartenstine said, "Mr. Bontempo," BT didn't move. He had his nose in a paperback. His long sandy hair fell like a curtain over his face. Mi-Su, sitting next to him, poked him with her fingertip. He toppled over and onto the floor. Everyone howled, but that wasn't the funniest thing. Once he was on the floor he kept reading for another ten seconds until he closed the book, looked up half-bewildered and said, "Huh?" More howls.

"Mr. Bontempo, front and center, please," said Mrs. Hartenstine.

So up he goes—the slowest walker you've ever seen—and you could tell he wasn't prepared. Not that that was a surprise; it would have been a shock if he *were* prepared. So he stood there, his paperback in his hand, cheap sneakers, hair flopping, giving us a loopy grin, like, OK, here I am, now what?

"We're waiting, Mr. Bontempo."

BT turned to the teacher. "Me, too." Not belligerent, just . . . BT.

More howls. It's not always easy to tell if BT is trying to be funny or not. Strangely, Mrs. Hartenstine has always cut him a lot of slack.

"Your poem," she said. "Time to recite."

BT pointed a finger in the air. "Ah!" He looked around the room, out the windows, back to the teacher. "And, uh, which poem was that again?"

Mrs. Hartenstine smiled. "'Stopping by

Woods on a Snowy Evening.' Does the name Robert Frost ring a bell?"

She smiled. Kids laughed. I think they were not just laughing at the scene in front of us. They were also laughing at the craziness of the situation, that the teacher actually expected Anthony Bontempo to be prepared.

BT looked out at us, like a character in a movie sometimes looks right at the camera and into the audience. It was comical. Obviously he hadn't given it a moment's thought. *You poor slob*, I was thinking, *when are you going to get it? How long do you think you'll survive in the real world?*

"You mean the one that starts, 'Whose woods are these I think I know . . . '?"

Stone silence.

Mrs. Hartenstine almost sang, "That's the one."

He folded his arms over his chest, holding the paperback with the cover facing out. It was *Crime and Punishment*. It was thick. Obese. I've never known a kid so totally unafraid of thick books. He closed his eyes and he recited Frost's poem. He said it in a monotone. He didn't try to make it interesting. He droned it out fast in half a minute and headed back to his seat, eyes and open mouths following him.

Something was wrong. I'm no poetry expert, but I knew something was wrong.

I think the teacher knew it, too. She called to him. "Mr. Bontempo?"

He looked up. He was already back into the paperback. "Yeah?" he said.

Mrs. Hartenstine blinked a few times. She seemed about to speak but she didn't. She merely smiled. "Never mind." She made a mark in her black book. "Next—Miss Bayshore."

I grabbed my textbook, flipped to Frost, found "Stopping by Woods." I read it through. The last line comes twice:

And miles to go before I sleep,
And miles to go before I sleep.

But that's not what BT had said. As Rachel Bayshore went on reciting her poem, it was BT's words I heard:

"And smiles to go before I weep,
And smiles to go before I weep."

44

I saw it as soon as I entered my room after school. My chess trophy stands on top of my bookcase by the door. And it was backward. The pewter king piece was facing the wall. Somebody had turned it around. Hilarious. I turned it back.

I didn't yell and scream and run after her. I used to, but it didn't do any good. I calmly walked down the hall to her room. Ozzie, her stuffed octopus, was on the bed. She was under the bed. The bottoms of her socks were showing. I just walked away, ignoring her. She hates to be ignored.

But during dinner I couldn't help myself. I glared across the table. "Don't do it again," I said. Calm. Cool. Not the least bit nasty.

She was building a snowman with her mashed potatoes. She was shaping it with a screwdriver. (Explanation: When Tabby first tried eating with one of my father's screwdrivers, my mother put a quick stop to it. But then my father got her her own set of plastic tools, and here's the deal: she's allowed to eat with them as long as she never uses them for anything else. So if you open our utensil drawer in the kitchen, you'll see a yellow plastic screwdriver, a pair of red pliers and a little blue saw along with the forks and spoons. And she's not allowed to eat with tools if we're having company. This excludes BT and Aunt Nancy, who are not considered outsiders.) So . . . she was working her mashed potatoes and pretending she didn't hear me.

"What did she do now?" said my mother.

"She messed with my trophy."

"Tabby? Did you?"

She looked up, like she didn't know what was going on. She's the world's worst actress. "Huh?" she said.

"Did you—" My mother looked at me. "What exactly did she do?"

"Turned it around."

Tabby quick clamped her lips shut, but not before she giggle-snorted into her potato snowman.

"See?" I said.

"Did you turn his trophy around?"

"No," she said. She would say no if I had

her on film. Unlike her hero, BT, she lies.

"Confess, pest," I said.

"Don't call her that," said my mother.

Tabby snarled, stabbing her screwdriver at me. "Yeah. Don't call me that."

There was a faint noise at the front door. We all turned to see a scrap of paper slipping onto the threshold. It was Korbet Finn, our next-door neighbor. Korbet is five. He's in love with Tabby. About once a week he delivers a love note to her this way.

Tabby ran for the note. She always hopes it will be from somebody else, anybody else, but it never is. She glanced at it, crumpled it, threw it to the floor, yanked open the door and yelled toward next door: "In yer dreams, lugnut!"

My father laughed. My mother looked at him. "Where does she get these words?"

"BT reads to her," I said. "Adult books."

Tabby slammed the door shut, kicked the note-ball into the dining room and stomped back to the table.

We needed to get back to the subject. "Just don't go near my trophy," I said.

Now Tabby was eating string beans with

her red pliers. Humming. Tuning me out.

I looked at my father for support.

He took a sip of coffee. "Leave Will's trophy alone, Tabby," he said. Reasonable. Gentle. Nonthreatening.

Tabby crushed a string bean with her pliers, then smashed the snowman. "I didn't do it!"

"Fine," said my father, calm, soft-spoken, forking into his meat loaf. "Just don't not-do it again."

Tabby exploded. "I didn't do it! I'm innocent!"

I snickered. "Yeah, right."

Tabby picked up a string bean and flung it in my face. "I hate you!" she screamed, and ran from the table, my mother snapping, "Tabby!" me hooting.

"Enough," said my mother.

My father said, "She's in rare form tonight."

After a while my mother said, "Here's my question. How could two such different children have come from the same parents?"

Sometimes I wonder that myself. I wonder why they had us so far apart. When I first heard that I was going to have a little brother or sister,

I wished for a brother. When they told me it would be a sister, I thought, OK, I can deal with that. I pictured myself giving her rides on my shoulders, teaching her to ride a bike.

Never happened.

Aunt Nancy says Tabby is just doing her job. That's what little sisters do: they pester. She says someday Tabby and I will be best friends. I say don't hold your breath.

I'm not saying I hate her. I don't. (Even though I do *feel* that way sometimes.) It's just that all we have are differences (age, gender, personality, etc.), nothing in common. Maybe when we're both adults we will get along. But for now, we lead mostly separate lives. If she didn't go out of her way to bug me, I'd hardly know she was around.

No one answered my mother's question. We ate in silence. Somehow the room seemed to be slowly revolving around the crumpled note-ball on the floor. In a dark crevice of a crumple I thought I saw a tiny sparkle.

Tabby made her daily phone call to Aunt Nancy. "I'm going to a star party!"

I still couldn't believe it. My parents were going to a play at Hedgerow. They had assumed I'd be playing Monopoly tonight. They assumed whether we played at Mi-Su's house or mine, I would babysit my sister. "No way," I said. "We're going to a star party at French Creek. Mi-Su's mother's driving us."

"Fine," she said, "Tabby goes with you."

"No way," I said.

"Tabby goes with you," she said.

Tabby gushed to Aunt Nancy, "I'm making a star shirt!"

She did. She got glitter and stars and pasted them all over a T-shirt. She thought it was a *party* party.

She called Aunt Nancy again. "It's for big people! There's gonna be appetizers! And kissing games! I'm gonna have coffee!"

▬ ▬ ▬

The tires crunched on the gravelly road.

"How do I know where it is?" said Mrs.

Kelly. "It's so dark."

"Look for the red lights," said Mi-Su.

"Where's BT?" said Mrs. Kelly.

"He doesn't care about stars," I said.

Up ahead—spots of red.

"Lights out," said Mi-Su.

The headlights went out.

Only the red spots were visible now. Some moving, some still.

The car pulled onto the grass, stopped. Three of us got out.

"Back at eleven," said Mrs. Kelly. "Watch Tabby." The car pulled away.

Tabby blurted, "Where's the party?"

I pointed to the sky. "Up there."

Tabby looked. "I don't see nothin'."

On the way Mi-Su tried to tell her that a star party is where people bring their telescopes to look at the night sky, but Tabby wasn't buying it. "Where's the pizza?" she whined.

"It's up there," I said. "Next to the Big Dipper. The constellation Pepperoni Pizza. The Greeks named it."

Mi-Su smacked my arm. "Stop it." She lifted Tabby to her shoulders and we headed for the party.

We could now make out shadowy figures behind the red spots, which were actually flashlights capped with red plastic. The Delaware Valley Astronomical Society has its star parties at French Creek because the light pollution is low there. This would be the last one until spring.

We wandered into the dark forest of telescopes. I'm always amazed at the size of the scopes.

Mi-Su and I split up. I told Tabby to go with Mi-Su, but she refused. She followed me. Not because she would rather be with me, but because she knew I didn't want her to.

Shadows drifted. Dull red circles bobbed and hovered. Whispers, but mostly silence, as if we were afraid to disturb the night. This was a place for stars, not people. A show. No button to click, no ticket to buy. Lean in to an eyepiece. Or just look up. The sky! It's been there all along! Someone pointed the light at himself: red floating face. Soft skitter of footsteps, excited whispers:

"What? *What*?"

"Saturn! *Rings!*"

"Where?"

"Over here! Come on!"

I was pumped. Mi-Su and I both want to be astronomers someday. I went from scope to scope, sampling, asking them what they've got.

"Moon. Great view of Sea of Tranquility."

"Mars."

"Jupiter. Four moons."

Reminded me of a summer fair: "Hey, right here, get yer moon! Yer stars! Three planets fer a dollah!"

Tabby tagging along, her finger hooked in my back belt loop, pestering every time I bent to an eyepiece: "Let me see!" If I didn't let her, she'd get loud. Sometimes I had to lift her, hold her while she squinted and whined, "I don't see nothin'!"

I'm not much interested in moons—ours, Jupiter's, whoever's. Going to Mars doesn't excite me. In fact, I'm pretty lukewarm about the whole solar system. For me, the farther away, the better. Stars. Galaxies. Quasars. That's what makes me tingle.

One monster scope had a line. I asked the

man-shadow at the end, "What?"

"Mars," he said. "You can see the polar cap."

I moved on.

Tabby yanked my belt loop. "I want to see Mars!"

I swung around, whipping her off her feet with her finger caught in the loop. She wailed, "Owww!"

"Don't be an infant," I snapped.

She roared: "I'm *not* an infant!"

The stars flinched. Shadows stopped. Gasps. Shushes.

I shook her. Her knobby shoulders were like golf balls. "Keep your voice *down*! Whisper!"

She whispered, "Ow. You hurt my finger."

To look at me, she had to tilt her head back as if she were looking at the sky. Sometimes I forget how tall I am to her. I saw moon gleam in both eyes. "You screamed like a baby. You want to be with grown-ups, act like one."

I continued my telescope hopping. I viewed a couple of nice star clusters. Most of all I wanted to see a galaxy, and finally it happened. There was a line of five people at a large scope. The lady at the end didn't even wait for me to ask. "Spiral galaxy!" she gushed.

The line went slowly. Tabby paraded up and down. "Want to see my star shirt?" She held back her arms and puffed out her chest. The paste-on paper stars glimmered in the moonlight. The gazers cooed and patted her on the head and asked dumb questions.

At last I reached the eyepiece. I couldn't see the target at first. Bright images swam by like fish. Then things steadied, and there it was. I could see the oval shape, the spiraling arms. It was the thrill of seeing it for real, the difference between seeing a fox in a zoo or a fox walking across a snow-covered field. But it was even more than that. It was the distance. The galaxy I was looking at, if it was anything like the Milky Way, contained at least a hundred billion (100,000,000,000) stars. "How far?" I said to the scope owner. "About two thousand." He meant two thousand light-years. Light travels 186,000 miles *per second*. In the time it takes me to say "per second," light zips around the world more than seven times.

So figure out how far light travels in a year (which has almost six *trillion* seconds), then multiply that by 2,000 for the distance to this spiral galaxy. How can something that big be so far away that it looks smaller than my little fingernail?

Pretty soon I knew all the scopes that were viewing galaxies, and so I just galaxy hopped. I was in heaven. I bumped into Mi-Su. "Ships passing in the night," she said. I said to Tabby, "Why don't you go with Mi-Su now?" "No," she said, only to bug me. I knew what I was going to say next time: "Stay with me. Don't go with Mi-Su." And she would go.

But we never got to next time. Somewhere along the line I realized I was no longer feeling the finger tug in my belt loop. I turned. She was gone. *She's off with Mi-Su*, I told myself and went on scoping.

But I couldn't concentrate, couldn't enjoy myself. What if she *wasn't* with Mi-Su? What if she was doing something stupid and getting herself hurt or whatever? I was the one who would get blamed. I was staring through an eyepiece at the Beehive Cluster, but all I could see was my sister wandering off among the dark shadows of strangers just to tick me off. I snapped back from the scope and stomped off. I stopped. I looked over the dark field, the starry horizon, the silent, moving shadows, the jutting shapes of the scopes, the dull red floating spots. I didn't know where to begin. I looked at my backlit watch: 10:30. Mrs. Kelly would be there soon, and I was missing wonders because I had to round up a stupid sister. I knew that one good call would do it. Just stand right there and rear back and bellow her name. But I couldn't. It would be like screaming in church.

I wandered, looking, listening. She's a chatterbox. Chances were I'd hear her before I saw her. But it was something else I heard. Two shadows and a bobbing red spot brushing past me, man and woman voices whispering excitedly. One word separated itself from the others: "Horsehead." I stopped in my tracks. I went after them. I'm not usually bold with people, but I just barged in: "Did you say Horsehead?"

"Yes," said the man. "It's unbelievable. I can't believe we saw it."

"Incredible," said the woman. "And I don't

know a star from a moon." She giggled. "He can die happy now."

I was breathing fast. "Where?"

The man pointed the flashlight, but of course the beam just puddled behind the red cap. "That way. Straight ahead. On the right. You'll see it. Big as a bathtub. On a trailer. Meade LX200." He wagged his head. They walked on.

I turned, walked. The Horsehead Nebula. It's, like, the Holy Grail. Mi-Su and I have been wanting to see it for years. I have a poster of it on my bedroom wall. We'd never seen it for real. It's a huge cloud of cold hydrogen gas and dust, way bigger than the solar system. It's visible because of starlit gases behind it, and it has the shape of a horse's head.

I didn't know what to do. Sister? Horsehead? Sister? Horsehead? My stomach felt like it was coming loose. And suddenly there it was, the monster scope, big as a bathtub, on a trailer behind an SUV—and the longest line I'd seen all night. Everybody wanted to see the Horsehead. It would take a half hour just to get to the head of the line, a half hour I'd gladly have spent, except for a missing sister. . . .

I wanted to cry, scream. I stomped off, spit hissing into the night: "Tabby! *Tabby!*"

At last I heard her voice, chattering away. I found her. She was with someone wearing an Indiana Jones hat. An old lady. "Well, hello there," she said. "You must be the big brother Tabby's been talking about." She held something out to me. "Like a snort of hot chocolate from my thermos here? We have an extra cup."

"No, thank you," I said. I was so mad I could hardly speak.

The old lady chuckled. "Your little sister had been hoping for coffee."

"She thinks she's twenty-one," I said.

Tabby piped: "Will, she has seven cats!"

"That's nice," I said. "Thanks for looking after her." I took the cup from Tabby's hand and gave it to the old lady. "We have to go now. Somebody's picking us up." I grabbed her hand and pulled her away.

She had to run to keep up. She squealed, "Where are we going?"

"To find Mi-Su."

She yanked on my arm. "I know where Mi-Su is!"

She wasn't lying. "Where?"

She wrapped her hand around my finger and pulled. "Follow me."

She wound among the dark shapes as if it were our own neighborhood. She led me out of the thicket of scopes and on toward a moonlit crest—and there she was.

No.

There *they* were.

It seemed to be one shape, one silhouette on the hill, but I knew it was two, and I knew who they were. Mi-Su and BT.

Tabby tugged. "Will, are they *kissing*?"

I turned away. Tabby yammered beside me, but I wasn't hearing, wasn't thinking, wasn't feeling. I don't remember the next few minutes. I only know that I was back among the dark shapes and glowing red spots. I checked my watch. It was time. We walked out to the gravel road. Mrs. Kelly's car was purring, parking lights on.

Mi-Su and BT were already in the car, Mi-Su in front, BT in the backseat. Tabby jumped in, climbed onto BT's lap, put his baseball cap on her head. I got in.

Mi-Su said from the front seat. "BT is crazy. He skateboarded all the way out here."

"I thought you didn't like star parties," I said.

"I was bored," he said. "It was a good night for a ride."

I waited a few seconds, then said it: "Somebody was showing the Horsehead."

Mi-Su screeched. "The Horsehead Nebula?" She whipped around to look at me. "You *saw* it?"

"No. There was a long line."

"Why didn't you come find me?"

"We did!" piped Tabby. "But you were busy kissing BT!"

The purr of the engine poured into the silence. Mi-Su shot a glance at her mother. "I was *not*."

"Yes, you were! You were! Wasn't she, Will? We saw you, on the hill!" Tabby was bouncing up and down on BT's lap.

More awkward silence.

Mrs. Kelly said, "Sounds like I better cover my ears."

More awkward silence.

We were leaving French Creek State Park, passing dark fields on the way to town. I saw tiny flashes beyond the fences, tiny sparks in the dark. It was late October. Wasn't it too late for fireflies?

PD30

I was in my room when my cell phone rang. She was calling about algebra homework. We talked about that and then she said, "You're acting funny."

"I am?"

"Yeah."

"So, why aren't you laughing?"

"You know what I mean. Strange. Different."

"I seem the same to me."

Silence. And from downstairs, the smell of my mother's famous Granny Smith apple pie.

Finally she said, "Is last night bothering you?"

"Why should it bother me?" I said.

"You tell me."

"Yeah, I guess it bothers me."

"I knew it."

"It bothers me that because of my sister I missed seeing the Horsehead. Who knows when I'll ever get another chance."

She laughed. "I knew it! I *knew* it! You're freaked out."

"Did I say that?"

"It's not about your sister or the Horsehead. It's about me and BT, that's what. We freaked you out."

The word "we" hit me like a dart. Tabby strolled by, stopped at my doorway, put on her snooty face, said, "Bob, you smell bad," moved on.

"What was there to get freaked out about?" *Wait—don't answer that.*

Too late.

"Oh, just him and me kissing, that's all."

"Wow, that's what you were doing? And here I thought you were watching the stars."

She laughed. "Good one, Will. No, as a matter of fact, we were kissing under the stars. As you well know."

"Actually, I was busy watching the stars. That's what they're for, I thought."

She paused. "Yeah. Sometimes. But sometimes they're for kissing under, too."

"Really? So that's what all those people were doing to their telescopes. Kissing them."

Tabby stopped in the doorway again, the faintest grin on her face. She stepped into my room, turned to the bookcase—the chess trophy—reached out with one pointed finger and tippy-touched the head of the king piece, grinning at me. I leaped from the bed. "Get out!" She screamed, ran.

"Good grief," said Mi-Su. "What's going on over there? Let me guess. Your adorable little sister."

"Bingo."

"So . . . as I was saying, stars are for kissing under."

"If you say so."

"I do say so. And here's where you're all wrong—it wasn't about me and BT."

"Did I say it was?"

She ignored me. "It was about me and BT and all the rest of it. The place. The night. The stars. Good grief, how could you *not* kiss some-body on a night like that?"

"If you're with Tabitha Tuppence."

She howled. "Touché. But really, it was the time and place more than the person. It just happened. He was there, I was there, that's all. I don't even remember . . . who . . ."

"—made the move?"

"Yeah. Who knows? Who cares? It was just, like, it's a crime to waste this moment. This moon. I would have kissed *anybody*."

"Glad I wasn't there."

Shouldn't have said that. I knew what was coming . . .

"Are you, Will?"

Saved by a *clack*! in the basement . . .

"Gotta go." I hung up. I raced down two flights of stairs, through the kitchen cloud of Granny Smith apple pie. Black Viper was in the middle of the basement floor, not where it was supposed to be.

The phone rang. It was still in my hand.

"What happened?"

"My sister was on my skateboard in the basement. She ran when she heard me coming."

The basement door was open.

"Crisis over now?"

I picked up Black Viper. "I guess."

She didn't speak again until I was back in my room. "Will?"

"Yeah?"

"I never told you—that was sweet of you to come looking for me to see the Horsehead."

"No big deal. I just thought you wanted to see it."

"I did. I do. When's the next star party?"

"Spring."

"Spring. Long time to wait."

"The sky's not going anywhere."

I got the feeling she wanted to say something, but there was only silence. Then: "Well, see ya."

"See ya."

I hung up.

Like a song on replay, the conversation kept running over and over in my head. It occurred to me that it's not true that the Horsehead isn't going anywhere. Actually, it's flying away at thousands of miles a second. Everything is. The Brimley clock. Mi-Su's smile. My mother's Granny Smith apple pie. We live in a silent explosion. Everything is flying away from everything else . . . flying away . . . flying away . . .

PD32

It's been over a month since BT became the first human to skateboard down Dead Man's Hill. No one else has tried it.

It's been three days since the star party. Since the silhouette on the hill. Was that a first for him also? Or has it been happening all along right under my nose? Exactly how much don't I know? Are others kissing her, too?

PD35

I ride Black Viper but I go nowhere. No matter what day it is, no matter what time, no matter where I am—I'm always at the star party, staring at the silhouette on the crest of the hill, wishing that one dark shape would split in two. But it never does.

PD44

Two Saturday nights have passed since the star party. We still play Monopoly as if two of the three of us have never kissed and a proton never died. BT comes late and buys everything he lands on and runs out of money. Mi-Su gives him loans and still he loses. We eat pizza and roll the dice and move the tokens around the board.

I keep looking for clues of something between them but I don't see any. Do they secretly meet? Since that one phone call, Mi-Su has clammed up. Is she afraid of hurting my feelings? Does she think I like her *that* way?

Do I?

I don't know.

I don't know.

I don't know.

PD49

The wheels of Black Viper crinkle over the autumn leaves.

PD55

I'm regressing. On Saturday mornings I go to the basement and do what I did when I was little: I watch Yosemite Sam and Daffy Duck cartoons. Tabby has discovered this, and so she joins me every Saturday morning. Here's how it goes. As I watch the cartoons I hear a sound behind me: *plink . . . plink . . . plink*. I know what it is. Jelly beans. Tabby is dropping them into the wastebasket, slowly, deliberately, so I'll hear. And not just any jelly beans. Black ones. Why? Because the only jelly beans I eat are the black ones, which I love. And so whenever she comes into some jelly beans, she heads for the wastebasket nearest to me and begins dropping the black ones: *plink . . . plink . . . plink*. Of course she's hoping that I'll turn and scream at her or something, but I don't. I just sit there and boil to myself, and when the last cartoon ends she runs up the stairs. The fact that she gives up her own Saturday morning cartoon-watching tells you all you need to know about how much she loves to torment me.

PD71

Top-floor dormer. Looking out the window. It was snowing. Well, just flurries actually. Thin dry flakes that weren't really falling but just sort of drifting by mistake into this Saturday in early December.

Our house has four floors, five if you count the basement. It looks pretty modern inside, but outside it's a big brick boxy thing with a porch that starts in front and goes around the side. It was built in 1913. The fourth floor is this one big dormer. It's cold in winter, hot in summer. It's my favorite part of the house. I come up here to be alone, to look out the window, to think. I call it dormer-dreaming.

We use the dormer as an attic. Out-of-season clothes. Junk. Christmas gifts are already piling up in the corner. I wonder if one of them is my atomic watch. I don't feel any temptation to sneak a peek. My parents love that about me. They know they could put a Christmas present on my pillow in July and I wouldn't open it until December 25. They could put that on my tombstone too:

HE COULD WAIT

My sister is another story. She has no more discipline than a shark smelling blood. That's why everybody's gifts are kept up here except hers. Nobody but my mother knows where they are. Tabby has already started pestering about them. She still believes in Santa Claus, of course, but she thinks, because she's so special, he dumps her stuff off at the house a month early.

There are other gifts up here, too, and that's a whole other story. They're mostly in silvery wrapping with silver ribbons. They're in a neat stack on a card table against the far wall, fifteen of them by actual count. They've been up here for eighteen years, since before I was born. Before that they were at Aunt Nancy's house. In the family, they're known as the wedding gifts.

My great-grandparents—Andrew and Margaret Tuppence—were missionaries. As the story goes, they met at seminary and fell in love. They got ordained and married on the same day. The next day they had to catch a boat to Africa, so there wasn't even time for a reception. But that didn't stop people from bringing gifts to the wedding. According to family legend, Margaret looked at the pile of gifts and laughed and said, "If I get any happier, I'll burst. We'll open them when we get back." She told her mother to take the gifts home with her, and off they went to Tanganyika, now known as Tanzania. Margaret and Andrew. This was in 1930.

Everyone expected them back in five years, ten at the most, but it just never worked out that way. Margaret and Andrew had two children over there, both boys, and they set up churches and medical clinics (Margaret was a medical doctor, too) and the years went by.

In 1943 Andrew died of black fever. Margaret stayed on with the boys. They finally came home in 1951. Margaret's mother, who was an old lady by then, still had the wedding gifts, but Margaret said she didn't want to open them without Andrew. "We'll open them together in Heaven someday," she said.

Well, Margaret's mother died, and then Margaret, and one of the boys became my grandfather and so forth, and the wedding gifts wound up at Aunt Nancy's and finally at our big old house, there on the card table against the wall in the dormer. For eighteen years they've been sitting there. They always look new because my mother keeps dusting them. She says they're history. They've become a sort of shrine, I guess. Some days in late afternoon the sun slants through the dormer window and nips a ribbon and it glistens like a tiny star.

Below the dormer window my sister was holding out her tongue and dripping Hershey's chocolate syrup onto it from a squeeze bottle. She turned her face to the sky. With the snowflakes falling on her chocolate-coated, stuck-out tongue, she figured she was getting an ice cream sundae.

And I wondered, as I often do when I'm in the dormer: *Why hasn't my out-of-control sister ever torn open the wedding gifts?*

I can see a lot from up there. I have my own telescope on a tripod. I slid it over to zero in on the clock on the tower of the Brimley Building. It was now an hour slow. I've noticed it seems slower every time I look. I'm surprised they're not doing something about it. I was about to focus in on Mi-Su's roof when I realized the snow was no longer thin flurries but fat, falling flakes. Beautiful.

All of a sudden I felt like I wanted to cry, which was really strange because I'm not the crying kind. Why did I feel so sad? The flakes were landing on the dry brown grass and Tabby now had a maraschino cherry on her tongue and her eyes were squeezed shut with her tongue out to the sky and she didn't know that Korbet Finn was sneaking up behind her.

I felt bad for Korbet because he loves her and he didn't know he was about to make a colossal mistake and he didn't know that all the way from the maraschino cherry to the farthest quasar protons were dying, the snow was falling and protons were dying across the universe and tears were streaming down my face and Korbet Finn was scooping snow from the dry grass and sneaking up on Tabby and I had to turn away and go downstairs because I didn't want to see.

PD77

We went to BT's house after school. It's a two-story dark green clapboard. The trim is supposed to be white, but the paint is mostly peeled off. The chimney is tilted as if it lost a battle with the wind.

But it's the inside that really gets your attention. When you open his front door you don't see a living room—you see a dump. Magazines stacked to the ceiling. Books, cereal boxes, cans, jars, soda bottles, bottle caps, clothes hangers, rubber bands, string, paper clips, candy wrappers, toothpaste tubes, spent balloons, old telephones, toasters, electrical cords and plugs, catalogs, movie tickets, telephone pole political posters, tin cans, sneakers, combs, jelly jars. Everywhere. Dining room table. Stairway. Bedrooms. Bathroom. It's like the whole house is an attic.

It's all Mr. Bontempo's idea. He's going to have a museum, he says. About twenty years from now, he figures, all this common stuff will start looking old and interesting. He says people will flock to his Museum of Yesterday, happy to pay admission so they can see what toilet paper wrappers used to look like. This is why there's a sign over the front door:

WHATEVER COMES HERE, STAYS HERE

As BT and I walked through pillars of stacked magazines, I heard snoring. A man was lying on the sofa. It wasn't BT's father.

"Who's that?" I whispered as we went up the stairs.

"Tom."

"Tom who?"

"I don't know."

"What's he doing here?"

"Sleeping."

I knew better than to ask more. Jelly jars, homeless people—Mr. Bontempo welcomes them all equally. Tom will probably hang around for a couple of days and next time I show up, he'll be gone. I've seen it happen before.

There are piles in BT's room, too, but of only one thing: books. They're crammed into a bookcase and stacked in piles alongside it, in front of it, in the corners of the room, on the windowsills. All paperbacks. He gets them for quarters and dimes at thrift shops and yard sales, for nothing on trash pickup days at curbsides. They're ratty, stained, many with no covers. He's a pack rat in training.

The rest of the room is pretty boring. No posters on the walls. No TV. No CD player. No computer. No dartboard. No trophies.

No pictures.

I thought I might see a picture of Mi-Su. I tried not to look obvious as I scanned the room for any sign of her.

Nothing.

Screams in the hallway. A flash of jeans and sneakers past the doorway. BT's little twin sisters. They're like chipmunks—darting, flitting. I never see anything but scraps of them. I don't think I'd recognize them by face in a police lineup.

BT went off to take a pee. I sneaked peeks under the bed, in the closet, in his dresser drawers. No sign of Mi-Su.

We talked for a while in his room. Tossed a tennis ball back and forth. I wanted to ask him questions, about the star party night, but he never gave me an opening, he never mentioned the night. Or her.

And then his father arrived. We could hear him pull up outside in a noiseball of squeals and chugs and a long, fading death rattle. He drives a truck. A big one, with slatted sides, like they haul mulch with. Somebody just gave it to him because it was junk and everybody knows Mr. B is The Human Dump. And a "piston magician," as he calls himself. So he fixed it up and now the truck is his ride.

He came up the stairs calling, "I smell

kids!" I thought of my father. Silent car. Silent entrance. I usually don't know he's home from work until I hear Tabby running and shrieking.

First through the doorway was a long-handled contraption that reminded me of a floor polisher, then came the brim of his cowboy hat, then his beaming smile. "My new toy," he said.

It was a metal detector. He's had them before. "New model?" I said.

"The newest. Pro Series VLF Discriminator. Eight-inch coil. We're hitting the beach this summer. Hundred dollars a day. Minimum."

He took a nickel from his pocket and tossed it under the bed. He put on earphones. He flipped a switch, the meter on the handle lit up. He swept the platterlike head of the detector under the bed. After a few seconds the needle on the meter leaped to the other side. I could hear a faint hum. He yipped: "Gotcha!"

So we went out to hunt treasure (Tom still snoring on the sofa). We piled into the truck and went bouncing through town on the way to Smedley Park. Mr. B kept up a constant chatter. I often wonder what it would be like to grow up as Mr. B's kid. (Amazingly, Mrs. B seems pretty regular. She runs the cafeteria at the hospital.) Mr. B doesn't work—I mean, regular nine-to-five work. His one steady job is—tah-dah!—newspaper boy. Every morning at five o'clock he zips around in his truck flipping papers onto driveways. After that, he could be doing anything: hauling furniture, painting houses, handymanning, fixing cars, planning his museum. It's not like he's never busy. It's just that from day to day—or, really, minute to minute—you never know what he's going to be busy *at*. Because even when he's working—fixing a car, painting a house—all he has to hear is "Daddy, come play!" and he's gone. He always has time.

HERE LIES
MARIO BONTEMPO
. . . FOR THE MOMENT

It's easy to see why BT blows through life like a candy wrapper in a hurricane. That's why, as much as I love Mr. B, I'm afraid that when I look at him I'm seeing a preview of who BT will become.

When we got to Smedley Park, Mr. B said, "Okay, Anthony, you want first crack at the Discriminator?"

"Sure," said BT.

Mr. B handed him the detector. "Go for it. Try the monkey bars. Upside-down kids. Falling money. Me and Will are gonna scout around a little."

BT nodded and put on the earphones and headed off, natural as you please. He never seems to be embarrassed about his father or his dumpy house or his ratty, off-the-junkpile skateboard.

We rode off. I figured by "scout around" Mr. B meant we would check out some curbside trash, looking for things for his museum. But we didn't. He pulled into a 7-Eleven parking lot and cut the motor. He took off his cowboy hat and laid it carefully on the dash. He turned to me and said, "So. Will. What's bothering you?"

I just sat there, stunned. All I could say was "Huh?"

He grinned. "Don't huh me. You've been the *Very* Big Think lately. It shows."

That's what he calls me sometimes: the Big Think. Because I always have this serious look on my face. It's not true, but that's what he says.

Maybe it was the way he leaned back against the cab door. Maybe it was the way he smiled and held out his hand, inviting, and said, "So . . . ?" Maybe it was knowing how safe Mr. B is to talk to. Maybe it was knowing that of the two things on my mind lately, the one I couldn't possibly talk to him about was Mi-Su.

Whatever, suddenly the words were tumbling out of my mouth: "I see tiny flashes." I knew how crazy it sounded, but he looked as if he heard people say it every day. I told him about Yellowknife and the proton that died. "It was seventy-seven days ago. I can't help keeping track."

I blathered on and on. I said things to him that I hadn't even said to myself. I asked him if he realized what it meant, the proton vanishing. Did he realize nothing would last, that sooner or later every last speck and smidgeon of matter would disappear?

He steepled his fingers under his chin. He nodded. "Interesting."

"See, here it is," I said. "I know I'm not going to live forever. I know that. I'm not stupid."

He nodded. "So?"

I chuckled. "So, I'm in the grave. Here lies Will Tuppence."

"And a fine lad he was."

"Yeah." Chuckle. "But here's the thing. Even though I'm dead, it's still me in there, in the coffin. It's still my stuff, Will Tuppence stuff. Will Tuppence's bones and calcium and molecules and atoms and protons."

He blinked, grinned, gave me a pistol fingerpoint. "For a while."

Sometimes I think he's read every book stacked in his house. "Yeah! Right! Okay! You're ahead of me." I was talking about the grimmest thing imaginable. Why was I excited? "You're thinking after eons of time even my coffin and bones will disintegrate and scatter and the sun will gobble up the earth and my protons will wind up in a star somewhere or just drifting through empty space."

He gave me wide-eyed wonder. "Did I say all that?"

I smacked his knee. "Absolutely. But see, even then, those particles were still me once. Somewhere in the universe, forever and ever, my protons—*my* protons—will be out there. *My* stuff."

"Will Tuppence was here."

"Exactly!" I loved him.

"But—"

"Yeah. *But.* But now we find out that stuff doesn't last. Not even protons. It *won't* be forever and ever after all. It'll be like I was never here. Never even here."

"Will Tuppence *wasn't* here."

"*But.*"

"Ah. The old double-but."

"*If* Heaven is a dimension, and angels are non-stuff, and Forever is . . . like, forever . . ."

He waited. "So? Then?"

"I'm afraid to say it. It sounds so goofy."

He tapped my knee. "No problem. I'll say it for you. If the second *but* is true, then maybe, somehow, in some form, you'll go on forever. Never-ending Will."

I winced. "It sounds even more crazy when somebody else says it. Why should I care what happens to my protons a gazillion years from now?" I turned to him. "Mr. B, what's wrong with me?"

He smiled. He squeezed my hand. "Nothing. You're smart enough to know you don't have all the answers, that's all."

"I'm god-awful at not being sure."

"You'll get better."

"But the tiny flashes—what about them?"

He gave a little chuckle. Wasn't he taking me seriously? "Are they like those little Fourth of July sparklers? Or those sparkling birthday candles?"

I nodded. "Both. And sometimes fireflies." I sighed. "I'm a nutcase!"

The neon lights of the 7-Eleven came on, giving his ears a green glow. He reached for his cowboy hat. "You're a kid trying to figure out the world you were born into, that's all. And I got news for you—you're no nuttier than me." He put the hat on. "Better get back to Anthony. He's probably rich by now." He turned the key. The truck rumbled to life.

PD78

Eureka!

I know BT's secret!

It came to me early this Saturday morning. I ran up to the dormer. I trained my telescope on the clock tower of the Brimley Building. It was now an hour and fifteen minutes slow.

I was right!

I called him up.

"You buffoon! You *total* buffoon!"

"Huh?" he said. Sounded like I woke him up.

"I know what you're doing. You're setting the Brimley clock back. You're doing it a little bit at a time."

Silence.

"Right?"

"Bingo. Good night."

"Don't ever try to keep a secret from me again," I said, but he had already hung up.

I try to imagine how he does it. I can't.

PD80

Mail was waiting for me when I got home from school. From Mr. B. Postal mail. He doesn't have a computer. I opened it. There were just three words:

Beware of solipsism

Funny word. Sounds like it means "love of melons" or something. I looked it up. It means believing that "the self is the only reality."

Am I a solipsist?

PD84

I'm going to kiss her.

It came to me during biology lab today. She was at another table, leaning over her fetal pig, and I couldn't stop staring at her. And somehow it was all the better because she didn't know I was staring. I don't know why, but I zeroed in on the back of her neck. Her black hair is short, so her neck shows, and it has this thin gold chain around it that holds her little amber sea horse, which at the moment was dangling over the fetal pig, and after years and years of knowing her, suddenly I couldn't take my eyes off the back of her neck.

I thought about her through the next class and I haven't stopped since. I think it will be OK. I mean, if she kissed BT, why not me? And I'm pretty sure (sometimes) there's nothing going on between them. No new jewelry has suddenly appeared on her. No sign of her in BT's room. No sneaky glances between them at Saturday-night Monopoly.

I keep thinking of what she said on the phone that day. I wrote things down:

" . . . wasn't about me and BT . . ."

" . . . the place . . . the night. . . the stars . . ."

" . . . I would have kissed *anybody* . . ."

I try not to think too deep into that one.

What I need to do now is come up with the time, the place. The moment. Too bad there are no star parties till spring. But there are still the stars. And light pollution. And clouds. Can't do anything about light pollution. Clouds, I can pray against. At least I can count on night to show up.

I'm thinking . . .

Thinking . . .

Letter from Mr. B:

Why does a back scratch feel better coming from somebody else than if you do it yourself?

Thinking . . .

Bingo! Christmas vacation. It's almost here. That's when I'll do it. I'm working on the details.

My mother is on the warpath.

Tabby found her Christmas presents, three days before Christmas. She tore the wrapping off every one. She knows everything she's getting.

They were hidden on the top shelf of the winter/summer clothes closet that my father had built in the basement. They were completely covered with summer shirts, bathing suits, etc. She had first tried standing on a chair, but she still couldn't reach. So she dragged the half stepladder down from the garage. Still not high enough. So she dragged down the full stepladder. Nobody knows how she did this without being seen or heard. (Or, I'm thinking, without help. I wonder if she lured Korbet. Or BT.)

My mother made the discovery around noon. It's like a crime scene. You can feel the frenzy. The chair and small stepladder flung across the basement. Summer shirts and bathing suits everywhere. The floor covered with ripped paper, bows, ribbons. Gift boxes ripped open, covers gone. One lid is twenty feet away, under the dartboard. So far there's no evidence that she actually took anything. It seems like she looked, then left everything there, in their boxes, on the floor, for all the world to see.

And my mother is calling: "TABBY! TABBEEEEE!"

PD96

I got it! The Exacta. My very own atomic watch. It doesn't look special. Just a gray plain-looking face with digital numbers, stainless-steel band. But its coolness lies beneath its looks. Its tiny receiver picks up the radio signal from the Atomic Clock, keeping me accurate to one second every million years. I wore it to bed Christmas night.

My parents punished Tabby by not rewrapping her presents. Her stuff sat under the tree yesterday in their boxes and plastic, looking naked next to everyone else's gussied-up gifts.

The idea was to teach her a lesson, teach her some self-control. Show her how she ruined the whole surprise factor of Christmas morning. So she won't do it again.

Memo: It didn't work. She tore into her stuff, paid no attention to the rest of us, shrieked and squealed and wallowed in her pile of no-bow presents like a hog in slop.

Actually, Tabby did get one wrapped present. From Korbet. He did his knock-and-run thing. Tabby didn't bother to answer the door, but my mother did. When she returned she said to Tabby, "There's a gift on the front step. I think it's for you." At that moment I could see Tabby's gears starting to work: How much do I hate Korbet? Enough to not even take his present?

By lunchtime she couldn't stand it any longer. She stomped out to the front step and snatched the gift. She flung it to the sofa. The wrap job was sloppy, scotch tape, no bows, no ribbons. It was the size of a deck of cards. In fact, I was sure that's what it was. Korbet is always asking her to play Old Maid.

Tabby pretended to ignore it, but you could

hear her brain grinding. About midafternoon she raced to the sofa, tore off the paper, saw it was a deck of Old Maid cards, snarled, "Lugnut!" and threw the cards into the wastebasket.

She did get cash from relatives. Forty-five dollars. She thinks she's rich.

PD97

Mi-Su is in Florida. She went down to visit her aunt and uncle in Tampa. This messes up my kiss plan. Got to retool.

PD100

One hundred days ago the proton died.

Tabby's Christmas money is gone.

In my sleep last night I heard the *plink* . . . *plink* . . . *plink* of Tabby dropping black jelly beans into a wastebasket.

I snapped.

I can't believe it. It's not me.

HERE LIES WILL TUPPENCE
HE NEVER SNAPPED
(WELL, MAYBE ONCE)

It happened tonight in my basement. Monopoly night. All the usual stuff: BT bought everything he landed on, BT ran out of money, BT mortgaged his properties, BT chirped, "Wheelin' and dealin'," BT went flat broke—nothing that hasn't happened a hundred times before. And then Mi-Su says to him, "How much do you need? I'll give you a loan"—like a hundred times before, only this time—*snap!*—I went bonkers.

It's like Will Tuppence II showed up. I heard myself yelling at Mi-Su: "No!"

Mi-Su winced as if my voice was a gust of wind. Her eyes went wide. "No what?"

"No more loans."

She laughed. "It's *my* money. I can do what I want with it."

"No, you can't." I groped for the rule book, riffled the pages. "Here! Quote, 'No player may borrow or lend money to another player.'" I smacked the page. "There it is."

She stared at me with those wide eyes, her mouth frozen in wonderment, as if she was seeing ten falling stars at once. "You're serious," she said. "Look at you. You're red."

Tabby clapped. "He's red! He's red!"

"Yeah, I'm serious," I tell her. "It's right here. In the rules."

"We break the rules all the time." She spoke softly, as if a loud voice would shatter me.

"It's not fair," I said. "It's not fair to the other players."

"You're the other player."

"We should play right or not play at all."

Mi-Su blinked. "Will, it doesn't make any difference. I just lend money to BT to keep him in the game for a little longer." Do you? I thought. Or is there some connection between this and the star-party kiss? "You *know* what's going to happen. Sooner or later he's going to lose. He *always* loses." She leaned forward, enunciated: "*And. He. Doesn't. Care.*"

All this time BT was lounging on the floor,

his chin propped up on his hand, grinning. Tabby jumped on his back. "Yeah! You always lose! Looozer! Loozer!"

"Well," I said, "maybe *I* care."

Mi-Su frowned. "What's that mean?"

I didn't know what it meant. The storm inside me had passed. Just dry husks of thought left on the ground.

"Maybe I'm thinking of him. Maybe I want him to win. Maybe I want him to win fair and square, that's all."

Mi-Su just stared. She knew it was all bull-crap.

BT finally spoke: "All I know is, you meatballs wouldn't stand a chance if this game had more railroads."

Tabby was perched on BT's shoulders. She pointed down at me, sneered, "Meatball!"

When I went to bed all I could think was: *You jerk. What makes you think she'll want to kiss you back now?*

Strange territory for me: the after-snap. I still feel myself vibrating. Humming. When I think about it, one minute I'm embarrassed, the next minute I'm—what? Excited? Thrilled? I mean, feeling myself lose it like that—I wonder if it was anything like BT's plunge down Dead Man's Hill: off the edge of self-control and down the slippery slope of my own words. Scary. Wouldn't do it again. But kind of OK with having done it that once.

And surprised that the whole world seems to be OK with it, too. No announcement over the PA this morning: "Calling all classes! Please note that on Saturday night at around nine o'clock Will Tuppence snapped. . . ."

BT was perfectly normal in school today, like it never happened. He came at me before homeroom: "Yo, Will! Check this out." And showed me a handful of change he found with his father's new detector. I had been toying with the idea of saying "Sorry about the other night," but I could see there was no point. He would have said, "What are you talking about?"

So he's letting me off the hook. Fine. But here's the twisted part: now I'm a little mad at *that*. Why? Because by ignoring my bad behavior he throws it back in my face. Because he refuses to care about *anything*. How do you deal with somebody who can't be insulted?

So what the heck do I want? I think I want him to forgive me. But that will never happen, because you can't forgive unless you first give a crap.

■ ■ ■

I finally got to Mi-Su at lunch. I steered her to an empty table in the corner. (BT usually sits with us, but he left school before lunch. Took a half-day. He does that sometimes.) Somebody called: "Check it out— Tuppence and Kelly." Mi-Su smiled (dazzling), laughed (smile on wheels), stuck out her tongue at the caller.

We sat down. I jumped in: "I was a jerk the other night."

She pried the plastic lid off her salad. "Just the other night?"

"Funny girl."

She went straight for the radish. She crunched it. "Did you tell him?"

I picked at the clear wrap on my egg salad sandwich. "Well, actually, I was sort of going to, and then when I saw him this morning he was so, like, Who cares? Like, it's *today* now. It's like he never even noticed."

I caught a whiff of radish breath. "He didn't."

I unwrapped my sandwich. "I feel like the villain."

"Hissss."

"I was thinking about this—"

"You're *always* thinking."

"The thing is, that's not why I get mad at him."

She crunched the second radish. "If you say so."

"Hey"—I jabbed half a sandwich at her—"maybe I care more about him than he cares about himself. Ever think of that? Ever think that when I bust his chops it's—"

She finished the sentence: "—for his own good. I know."

"So?" I said. "Is that so bad? Is it so bad to want him to amount to something? Look at him. He goes down hills and messes up clocks. What kind of life is that?"

She sipped her orange juice. Orange juice and radish. Sicko. "What I think is, we have this conversation about once a month."

"Sorry," I said. "So, shoot me for caring."

Now she was looking at me funny.

"What?" I said.

"It just occurred to me. Out of the blue."

"*What?*"

"You never laugh out loud."

"You're off the subject," I told her. "And you're crazy, too. I do so laugh out loud."

She studied me. "I don't think so. I've known you most of my life. If you did, I'd know it."

"Well, you're wrong."

She shaded her eyes with her hand and squinted, as if I was standing in sunlight far away. "No, I don't think so." She brought back her normal face, smiled. "Anyway, I think you should just stop caring. So much."

"Huh?"

"He's got parents for that. Just be his friend."

"I am. He's my *best* friend. That's what this is all about."

"You have a funny way of showing it. And anyway, you're not caring. You're meddling."

Am I? Is she right?

"Don't *you* care about him?" I said. And instantly wished I could take the words back. They covered more territory than I meant. Would she think I was thinking of the star-party kiss?

But she was cool. Impy. Mi-Su. She plastic-forked salad into her mouth, chewed, stared at me, fingered the amber sea horse at her throat, grinned. "Of course."

What did she mean by that?

"So?" I said. Whatever that meant.

"So," she said, munching, "I'm along for the ride." The bell rang. She laughed, pointed at my sandwich. "You never took a bite, you moron."

— — —

The Big Snap has knocked me off my planning for the kiss. I need to refocus.

PD109

Along for the ride . . . along for the ride . . .

PD110

Looking in the mirror. Smiling. Laughing out loud.

PD111

plink . . . plink . . . plink . . .

PD113

I'm at the top of a hill. Dead Man's Hill. Black Viper wobbles beneath me. Wind whistles. I'm scared. Nothing but air beneath me. I want to go back but I can't. Something pushes me. I spill off the edge, I'm heading down. I can't stop. There's nothing to hang on to. My body drags back while my toes point straight down like a ballet dancer. Black Viper's wheels are stuttering, skipping. The wind is screaming. I can't stop. The wheels lose contact. I'm surfing space. Black Viper goes drifting off, like a jettisoned fuel tank. I'm falling . . . falling . . . the wind is screaming . . . *Wally ate a potato every day . . . Wally ate a potato every day . . .*

I opened my eyes.

Tabby was straddling my chest, wearing her snooty I-can-read face, saying over and over, "Wally ate a potato every day."

I bucked, I swatted, but she was faster. She flitted from the bed like a grasshopper. On the way out the door she bumped the bookcase. My chess trophy tottered, toppled, crashed to the floor.

The pewter King Arthur lay by himself, broken off at the ankles. I cradled it in my hand. The only trophy I'd ever won.

PD118

The trophy is fixed. I got it back from Hicks' today. It's not on the bookcase by the door anymore. It's high. On top of my dresser.

I put a hook-and-eye lock on my door. I use it at night.

PD119

Valentine's Day! Perfecto! That's when I'll do it.

I'm drawing up a plan.

PD120

Saturday. The dormer. BT and me.

He had to take his little twin chipmunks to the dentist. Then they came here. They were all playing in Tabby's room, the three of them shrieking beneath us.

We sat on the floor, eating hoagies from

the deli. BT pointed to the wedding gifts. "When are you gonna open them?"

I shrugged. "Me? Never. Maybe nobody ever will. Or maybe some archaeologist some-day."

He wagged his head. "Crazy."

"Why?"

"They're both dead, right? The newly-weds?"

"Yeah. Andrew and Margaret. Long dead."

"So open them."

"They're not mine. They're like a memorial. It's a family tradition to *not* open them."

"Open them."

"No."

He reached. "*I'll* open them."

I slapped his hand away.

"If they were in my house—"

"Yeah," I said, "I know."

"I'm surprised Tabby hasn't ripped into them."

"Yeah," I said, "I am, too. It's a mystery."

It seemed impossible that the shrieking below could get any louder, but suddenly it did, followed by stampeding footsteps. Three miniature girls burst into the dormer. The first, one of the twins, raced bawling into BT's arms.

"Tabby tripped me!"

"She stold Ozzie," gushed Tabby. "I had to stop her." She was hugging her octopus.

"Where's it hurt?" said BT.

"I don't *know*!" wailed the twin. Her arms collared BT's neck, her face was buried under his chin. I'd never heard such screaming. I kept looking for blood. Tabby and the other twin were gaping.

BT cradled her like a baby, rocked her. He was perfectly calm. "I think I know," he said. He pulled up her pant leg. "I think it's right here." He kissed her knee. "That better?"

She nodded. She stopped bawling. He tickled her. She laughed. A minute later the three of them were shrieking again in Tabby's room.

PD127

Eighteen days till Valentine's! I work on The Plan every day. It's almost ready.

PD128

Planning . . .

PD129

Planning . . .

PD130

<u>THE PLAN</u>

Inspired by the words of Mi-Su Kelly:
"The stars. The place. The night."

I. The Place
   A. Smedley Park
       1. Picnic grove
II. The Night
   A. Speaks for itself
III. The Stars

A. First Option (Clear Sky)
    1. Real (Polaris, Sirius, etc.)
B. Second Option (Cloudy Sky)
    1. Not real (See V-B)

IV. Extra Credit
  A. The Moon

V. Equipment/Materials
  A. Thermos
    1. Hot chocolate
  B. Paper Stars
    1. Possible supply sources
      a. Lily Pad Art Supplies
      b. Staples
      c. Rite-Aid

VI. The Bait (at school, February 14)
  A. "I'm taking my telescope to Smedley Park tonight. Try to see the Horsehead Nebula. Want to come?"

VII. Procedure
  A. Walk with her to Smedley Park after dinner
  B. Set up scope
    1. Fail to find Horsehead Nebula
      a. On purpose
  C. Drink hot chocolate
    1. Share cup

2. Romantic
D. Words
    1. "Hey, I guess we're having our own little star party here, huh?"
    2. "Know what we need? More stars!"
E. Dump paper stars over our heads
F. Words
    1. "Happy Valentine's Day!"
G. Kiss

PD132

I bought stars today at Lily Pad. Little gold ones, like I used to get on my spelling quizzes in first grade. I also bought hot chocolate. Microwavable. With little marsh-mallows.

PD133

This is the month! Thirteen days and a wake-up.

PD136

The more I look at The Plan, the more I see what it doesn't cover: What happens after the kiss? How will she react? What will she say? I keep coming up with new possibilities. All day long I hear her voice in my head:

"Oh, Will!"

"Will . . . I didn't know you felt that way about me."

"Those stars did the trick!"

"I wish you hadn't done that, Will."

PD137

"**Y**ou Romeo, you."

"Mmm . . . yummy."

"I've had better kisses from a puppy."

PD139

One week!

"**W**ill . . . wow! Who have you been practicing on?"

"Kiss me again, you fool."

"Not bad—but you're no BT."

I was tense at Monopoly tonight. All the usual little things—Mi-Su calling me "sicko" because of my anchovies and extra sauce, BT yapping he's "wheelin' and dealin'"—seemed a little different, dipped in glitter, like this is our last Saturday-night Monopoly game before the world changes—again. I remembered Mi-Su's words when the proton died: "Nothing will ever be the same."

I watched BT move the tiny iron around the board, and suddenly the question occurred to me: *Am* I *cheating on* him*? How much do I really know about him and Mi-Su? Mi-Su says it was the night, not BT. Is she telling the truth? Even if she* *is, what about BT? Was it just the night and the stars for him, too? Or was it Mi-Su? Has he been thinking about Mi-Su just like I have? Has he discovered the back of her neck, too?*

PD142

Something could have happened.

But didn't.

Around seven o'clock tonight the doorbell rang. It was Mi-Su. I don't know why, but I was shocked. She just stood there smiling: black coat, bright red knitted hat with bunny-tail tassel, matching red mittens, matching red nose from the cold, just standing there smiling at me, breaking the world record for adorableness. I didn't think—I just did. I reached out and grabbed her and kissed her right there on the front step. . . .

Hah! I wish.

Mi-Su really did come to the door, but it was only a kind of second me—Shadow Me—that reacted that way. Real Me just stood there, because making a move now wasn't in The Plan and there were still three days to go. Real Me smiled back at her and said, "Hi. What's up?" and she made a face and said, "Geometry. I hate it. Can you help me?" and Real Me said, "Sure, come on in."

She stayed for a couple of hours and we did her geometry, and most of the time we were alone in the basement and sometimes her face was only inches from mine, and Shadow Me kept kicking Real Me in the shins and hissing, "Kiss her . . . kiss her *now*! . . ." but I stayed with The Plan, and when I went to bed the pillow whispered in my ear, "You blew it."

PD143

"Nice try, for an amateur. Come back and see me in a couple of years."

Along the flagstone walkway that goes from our driveway to the front door, there are bushes. I was coasting down the sidewalk after school, about a block from home. Tabby's school bus stopped and out she popped. She trudged up the driveway, her backpack hugging her like a baby monkey. She was almost to the front step when suddenly the bushes moved and out popped Korbet Finn. "Happy Valentine's Day!" he shouted and planted a nose-deep kiss in her cheek.

Tabby recoiled, snarled, "That's tomorrow, lugnut!" and shoved him back into the bushes.

Uh-oh. Was this an omen for tomorrow— The Big Day?

I'm going to chicken out. I know it. I'm terrified. My atomic watch is ticking off the seconds. I can't do it. I don't like not knowing what comes after Plan Part VII-G. In chess, you don't make a move until you know how your opponent will counter. I'm going to chicken out!

The night was clear. No clouds. The stars as good as they get around here. Even the moon showed up, but just a thin toenail clipping, not bright enough to drown out the stars.

I set up my scope. Couldn't find the Horsehead. (Aw shucks.) Let her try. No dice. Her disappointment was no act. "Poopy!" she said. I don't know why, that just tickled me. We drank hot chocolate from the same thermos cup. The red plastic cup matched her mittens and hat. I had been afraid she would say, "Didn't you bring a cup for me?" but she didn't.

When we finished the hot chocolate, I screwed the cup back on and walked a couple of steps away from her and pretended to gaze up at the sky and said, "Hey, guess what?"

"What?" she said.

"I think we're having our own little star party here."

After I said it I didn't breathe, because I was sure she was going to say, "Are you *kidding*? This isn't even *close* to a *real* star party at French Creek. So don't get any *ideas*, pal."

But she didn't.

She looked at me. She looked at the sky. She held out her arms as if welcoming the stars to come down. She said, "Well . . . yeah . . . you're right."

I reached into my pocket (where I had dumped the paper stars before I left the house). I walked over to her. Even with the real stars up there, I was going to use all my ammo. I swallowed hard. "Know what we need?" I said—croaked, actually.

"What?" she said dreamily, looking up.

I froze. My hand was in my pocket and the stars were in my hand, but I couldn't move, I couldn't speak.

And then she seemed to come out of her trance and her face was turning toward me and her mouth was opening to say something and suddenly I was doing it—holding my fistful of stars over her head and letting them fall and blurting way too loud, "More stars!"

And "Happy Valentine's Day!"

And kissing her.

So hard that my teeth clacked into hers. I

backed off and it was soft and OK and her shoulders were in my hands and I only knew what I could feel because my eyes were clamped down shut. When I finally pulled away and opened my eyes, I was surprised to see that hers were closed, too.

I braced myself for her words—*Please don't wisecrack*, I prayed—but she said nothing. She just smiled. And kissed me again.

We were halfway home when I realized I had left my telescope behind and we had to go back for it.

PD147

On Fridays the first time I see Mi-Su is in second-period Spanish. I'm always there first. I take a seat toward the back. She's always one of the last to come in. She looks for me, smiles, waggles her fingertips and takes a seat in the first row, even though there's usually an empty seat beside me.

I thought today might be different. I

thought she might come back to the seat beside me. She didn't. Everything was the same: look for me, smile, waggle, first row. Well, what did I expect? Did I expect her to rush back and flop into my lap? Did I think she'd be hauling around a big sign saying WILL KISSED ME LAST NIGHT?

Stupid me, maybe I did, because I kept turning corners all day, half expecting to bump into her, smiling, maybe winking, shyly/slyly saying something. Instead of thinking about Spanish and physics and English, my head ran imaginary conversations:

Her: Hi.

Me: Hi.

Her: Nice time last night.

Me: Yeah.

Her: I didn't sleep much.

Me: Me neither.

Her: I kept thinking about . . .

Me: What?

Her (sly grin): You know.

Me: Yeah.

Her: Know what I wish?

Me: What?

Her: I wish a whole year passed already and this is Valentine's Day again.

Me: Yeah.

Her: So when are you going to kiss me again?

▬ ▬ ▬

Lunchtime—not the one in my head but the real one—was a dud. She talked to me. She talked to BT. She talked to the other kids at the table. She didn't send me any special, secret smiles. No winks. No mention of Valentine's Day. No leading questions to the others, like, "So, what did *you* guys do last night?"

Nothing.

So after lunch I started asking myself leading questions. Like, *Did Mi-Su say anything to BT about last night?* Like, *What?*

Suddenly I wanted to check out BT for clues. I tried to remember. Was he looking at me funny today? Did he seem a little frosty? I couldn't check him out now because he took another half-day. When lunch was over, instead of going to his next class, he just kept walking right on out of school.

I started running a new conversation in my head:

Her: So, what did you do last night?

Him: Nothing. Hung at home. Read. You?

Her: Went to Smedley.

Him: At night?

Her: Yeah. With Will.

Him (taken aback): Our Will? Will Tuppence?

Her: No, Will Shakespeare.

Him: Wha'd you do?

Her: Drank hot chocolate. Looked at the stars. He brought his telescope.

Him: What else?

Her: He kissed me.

Him: Did you kiss him back?

Her: I guess you could say that.

Him: Did you like it?

Her: I guess you could say that.

Him: Do you love him? Is that what it is now, Will and Mi-Su forever?

Her (laughs): Hey—the place. The night. The stars. How could you *not* kiss somebody?

Him: What about us? You, me, the star

party? Was it as good as that?

Her (sly grin): Wouldn't *you* like to know?

— — —

By last class I was a mess. Did she? Didn't she? And then school was over and I was heading for the exit when I felt someone squeeze my hand. She was rushing past me, saying, "Gotta run!" I knew she was heading for the auditorium and tryouts for *The Music Man*. I felt that squeeze all the way home. I feel it now. It says everything. *Yes!*

PD148

I was right: the world *has* changed. I'm just not sure exactly how.

We were at Mi-Su's for Monopoly. I went over early. I figured we could fit in a little alone-time together. And so who answers the door? BT! He was already there. He's never early. Late is the only thing he ever is. That's his middle name: Late. BLT, I call him sometimes.

Words jammed in my head: *Why are you early? Do you know about me and Mi-Su the other night? What did she say to you? What's going on here?* The words that came out were: "You're early."

"So are you," he said. He reached for the pizza boxes I carried. "Gimme. I'm hungry."

An hour later BT went up to the bathroom and Mi-Su and I found ourselves alone. At first neither of us said a word. I snuck a glance at her. She was counting her money. Finally I reached out and touched her hand with the tip of my finger and said, "Hi." Her head came up with that dazzling smile. She did the same fingertip thing to my hand. "Hi." And suddenly everything was okay. Perfect.

"How did the tryouts go?" I said.

"Good."

"Did you make it?"

"Everybody makes it. It's just a question of what role you get."

"What role do you want?"

"Well, every girl wants to be Marian."

"Who's that?"

"The female lead. The librarian. She gets to sing all the great songs."

"That'll be you."

She laughed. "No, it won't be me. It'll be some senior. Probably Jen Willard. I'll be in the chorus. I'll be happy."

And then BT came back and resumed buying up railroads and "wheelin' and dealin'," mortgaging to the hilt, went broke and on his next move landed on Chance. Picked a card. Advance to Illinois Avenue. He slid his thimble down to Illinois, which I owned. At this point I only had two houses on it, so all he owed me was $300, but it might as well have been three million. I said, "Three hundred," and Mi-Su burst out laughing.

"What?" I said.

"You," she said. "The way you said it."

Already I didn't like how this was going.

"How many ways are there to say three hundred?"

She laughed again. "I don't know. You say it so . . . casual. So businessy. Like you expect him to pay it. Like you don't know he's totally broke."

I turned to BT. I tried to sound as mournful as possible. "I regret to inform you, sir, that a rental fee in the amount of three hundred dollars is now due."

BT held out his hands, wrists together to be cuffed. "Take me to the poorhouse."

"Not yet," said Mi-Su. There was a new firmness in her voice. I expected her usual Operation Rescue BT, but this time it was different. She didn't give him the $300; she handed it directly to me. She looked me in the eye, smiled, daring me to say something. And she wasn't finished. She picked up her yellow title deed cards—Atlantic Avenue, Ventnor Avenue, Marvin Gardens—and plopped all three down in front of BT. Plus the houses she had built on them.

I was practically biting my tongue in half.

She arched an eyebrow. "You say something?"

I shook my head. "Nope."

"You're not going to reach for the rule book, are you?" She was grinning.

I pled ignorance. "Rule book? Me?"

"Because this isn't money, you know. It's property. And it's not a loan. It's a gift. It's"—she beamed her smile on BT—"charity."

"*Hot* dog!" piped BT. He put the green houses on the yellow properties. "Wheelin' and dealin'."

Mi-Su was now wearing her I'm-so-sincere face. "We're not breaking any rule book rules here, are we, Willy?"

She knows I hate that name. "Not that I can see."

"Because we sure don't want to break any rules, do we, Willy?"

"Can't have that," I said.

There was more than Monopoly going on here, but I didn't know what it was. I had a feeling that if I said the wrong word, she would leap across the board into his arms and shout out: "He's the one I want!"

The game, if you can call it that, played out. BT, even with his windfall "gift," still managed to blow it all and wound up broke as always. After that, Mi-Su made a string of stupid moves and declared bankruptcy. "You win, Will," she said cheerily.

Walking home, I wondered who the real winner was.

PD149

I'm dreaming. I'm standing behind Mi-Su. I know there's a smile on her face but I can't see it. I want to tell her to turn around. I keep trying but I can't speak. I can feel my throat getting sore. And now something is coming out of my mouth, but it isn't words. It's tiny flashes. A glittery stream of them. Protons leaving me flying and dying into her black hair.

PD151

She was right. She didn't get the role of Marian the librarian. She doesn't care. She's in the chorus, a citizen of River City. She gets to sing and dance.

"I can't wait," she said.

"Won't you be nervous?" I said.

"Probably," she said.

She sang a few notes. I clapped. She bowed. She threw out her arms. She blurted, "I love it!"

Monopoly. My house. I told Mi-Su if she came over early we could play a little chess. Still maneuvering for alone time. So here she was, with the pizzas. Of course, Tabby was here, too, but I had that problem covered. I had lured her upstairs with *Finding Nemo* on the DVD player.

So we were alone in the basement, but my mind wasn't on chess. It was where it's been since this new idea came to me yesterday. I moved a bishop. I yawned, acted casual. "Hey," I said, "I just thought of something."

"What?" she said, mulling over her next move.

"*Goop* is playing at the Cineplex."

"Yeah?"

"Yeah." Deep breath . . . casual . . . casual . . . "Wanna go?"

"Okay."

"So I was thinking next Saturday? Instead of Monopoly?"

"Okay."

Yes!

I wasn't happy for long. BT arrived. Tabby heard him and abandoned Nemo and we were all standing there and hadn't even opened the pizzas when Mi-Su says to BT, "We're going to the movies next week instead of Monopoly."

"Yeah?" he said. "What are we gonna see?"

"*Goop*."

Tabby shrieked. "Ooo! Ooo! Can I come?"

"It's scary," said Mi-Su. "You're too little."

Tabby stood at attention. "I'm not little. I'm big." She flopped into Mi-Su's lap. "Please! *Pleeeeeze!*"

"You *are* little! You're not even in first grade! You're an infant!"

I wondered who was shouting—and realized it was *me*. Everyone was staring. Tabby was clinging to Mi-Su. Snap #2.

Hey, listen, sorry about that. Tabby just got caught in the crossfire. She's not the one I'm mad at. I'm mad at you, BT. And you, Mi-Su. Because when I said WE *could go to the movies, the* WE *meant you and me. Not you and me* AND *BT.*

That's what I was thinking, but I didn't say anything.

Mi-Su reached down over Tabby and counted out the money for her hotel. "Well," she said, "that was quite the outburst. And a waste. The fact is, big girl"—she tweaked Tabby's nose, Tabby giggled—"your mother isn't going to let you go anyway." She handed the money to me. I'm always the banker. She wasn't smiling.

Am I losing Mi-Su already?

PD156

I'm afraid she's never going to smile at me again.

PD157

She did! As we passed in the hallway on the way to first period. And in algebra and

129

English. And at lunch. She smiled and talked and everything seemed normal.

I don't see her much after school anymore. She's busy rehearsing for *The Music Man*.

PD158

Imaginary conversation with BT:

"You're still my best friend, OK?"

"OK."

"Always will be."

"Ditto."

"But listen, this movie coming up Saturday night—it was supposed to be just me and Mi-Su."

"Really? OK. I didn't want to go anyway."

"No, wait, let me explain. I mean, in my mind I was asking her for a date. Me and her. To the movies. OK? See, like, things are different now. I mean, we're all still friends, I'm not saying we're not. It's just that, well, on Valentine's night we—by 'we' I mean Mi-Su and I—we went to Smedley Park and I kissed her and she kissed me back and it was, y'know, special. I mean, something sort of started between us. I really like her. I mean, as a girlfriend. I keep thinking about her. That's why I asked her to the movies. And now it's, like, the three of us, and I just thought maybe you ought to know that Mi-Su and I have this thing going—OK, *I* have this thing going, I'm still not sure about her—and, well, if you, y'know, like, decided you couldn't make it Saturday night for some reason and Mi-Su and I had to go to the movie all by ourselves, alone, just the two of us, well, that would, like, be OK."

"OK."

"Uh, OK what?"

"OK."

PD163

Sunday. In the dormer. Alone with the wedding gifts. Still trying to figure out what happened last night.

Mrs. Kelly drove us to the Cineplex. Mi-Su sat between me and BT in the backseat. Mrs. Kelly, the jokester, said, "No hanky-panky back there." A minute later Mi-Su piped up, "Mom! They're *both* trying to kiss me!" A few more minutes of nonsense, and then BT went to sleep. He does that a lot. He stays up all night and then nods off at odd times.

Mrs. Kelly dropped us off. The plan was for her to pick us up at eleven at the nearby Pizzarama. Glory be!—BT paid for his own ticket. And then whipped out a ten-dollar bill. "We went detecting last night," he explained. A bucket of buttered popcorn and Peanut Chews and the bill was gone.

Ten minutes into *Goop* BT says, "This sucks."

"It's just getting started," I said. "Give it a chance."

We were all dipping into the bucket of popcorn, Mi-Su between us. She held the bucket. Sometimes all three of our hands were in it.

Five minutes later BT says, "I'm leaving." He starts to get up.

Mi-Su clamps down on his arm. "No."

I'm thinking: *Yes!*

And wondering: *Why doesn't she just let him go?*

"It stinks," said BT. "It's a scary movie that isn't scary. It's not even funny."

Mi-Su nodded. "It does stink. I'm going, too." She turned to me. "Will?"

"What?" I said.

"Coming?"

Her eyes were glowing from the screen.

"You're really going?" I said.

"Yeah. Come on."

"We just paid money."

"Money schmoney. Come on."

Her glowing eyes were staring into mine.

"Stay," I said.

On the other side of her, BT popped up— "Bye"—and headed up the aisle.

"Coming?" said Mi-Su.

"No," I said.

"Bye," she said. She handed me the bucket of popcorn and took off.

I was stunned. Numb. It had all happened so fast, out of nowhere. I kept seeing her hand clamped on his arm. Her last words: "Coming?"

and "Bye." She knew I wanted to stay, and she knew he wanted to go. She picked him. Instead of saying "Coming?" why couldn't she have said, "Will, come on. Please. We don't want to go without you. *I* don't want to go without you." But no. It was like an ultimatum: Coming? . . . No? . . . Bye. No hand tugging on *my* arm.

This time a week before, I had pictured her sitting in the movie beside me, maybe my arm around her, or holding hands, in our own little world. And now they were outside, the two of them, together, and I was inside, alone. How did it happen? Have I been kidding myself all this time? Have she and BT had a thing going all this time and I was just too dumb to see it? Is that why she included him in my movie date? I saw her kissing him with my own eyes at the star party. Why did I believe her when she said it wasn't about BT? And what about Valentine's night? Was she just feeling sorry for me? Tossing me a crumb?

I thought: *She didn't exactly bend over backward trying to get you to come along. Maybe they're happy you stayed behind. You don't want to go anywhere you're not wanted, do you? Wake up, stupid—they probably planned this whole thing.*

But on the other hand . . . she did look into my eyes and say, "Coming?" And she did squeeze my hand in school the day after Valentine's.

Up on the screen the Goop was sliming under a doorway, oozing up a bedsheet and into the nostrils of a sleeping girl. I bolted from my seat. Popcorn flew. I rushed out of the theater.

They were gone.

The Cineplex is in an outdoor shopping center called Edgemont Plaza. There's a Main Street, tall lantern-style lamps, brick side-walks, neon. It's supposed to look like an old-fashioned downtown. This being early March and still cold, there weren't a lot of people outside. I started walking. Up and down Main Street. Around the parking lots. Behind the stores. I aimed for the shadows, the crannies. I kept expecting to bump into them making out behind some SUV or Dumpster. And if that did happen, what would I say? "Oh, hi! Mind if I watch you make out? . . . Mind if I join you?"

If I caught them, what would she say this time? "The place . . . the night . . . the neon"?

I was getting frantic. I was kicking myself for not leaving the movie with them.

I peered into the windows of restaurants, ducked into stores. I found her in Barnes & Noble. In the café section, eating a little round chocolate Bundt cake, her favorite food in the world. She was washing it down with a latte. No BT in sight.

She saw me coming. She waved me over. "Hi!" She seemed sincerely happy to see me. I sat down.

"So how was the movie?" she said.

I didn't want to tell her what I had really been doing for the last hour. "You were right," I said. "It stunk."

"You should listen to us next time."

"Yeah."

Us.

"So," I said, "where's your boyfriend?"

I don't know why it came out that way.

She didn't skip a beat. She didn't raise her eyebrows. She didn't say, "What boyfriend?" Or, "What are you talking about?" Or, "You mean BT? He's not my boyfriend, silly you."

She just chuckled and said, "Sleeping."

"Oh," I said, and then not much else as she ate her cake and gabbled on about *The Music Man* and the cast and how much fun rehearsals were. Finally she drained the latte and said, "Okay, time for pizza." Mi-Su outeats everyone I know. "I have one regret in life—" she said. She licked her fingertip and used it to pick cake crumbs from the table. I thought of an anteater's tongue flicking and picking off ants.

"What's that?" I said, not sure I wanted to know.

She pushed her chair back, stood. "There's no such thing as chocolate Bundt cake pizza."

I smiled, but I knew she wasn't kidding. I once saw her dip a ham sandwich in chocolate pudding.

BT was zonked out in an easy chair, sprawling, arms flopped over the sides, legs straight out and propped on his heels, mouth open, face to the bright ceiling lights. And snoring. In a facing chair, a lady with a magazine glared at him.

"He your friend?" said the lady.

Mi-Su acted surprised. "Me? Oh, no. He must be a bum off the street."

Now the lady was glaring at Mi-Su. "If you don't get *your friend* out of here, I'm going to the manager."

"Uh-oh," said Mi-Su. She tickled BT's stomach. He snorted. His eyes opened a crack. "Come on, Sleeping Beauty. Nap time's over." She took him by both hands and dragged him to his feet. "Follow us."

BT zombied after us. When we hit the fiction stacks, Mi-Su looked back at the glaring lady and whispered, "Grouch."

So we ate at Pizzarama and Mrs. Kelly picked us up and Mi-Su sat between us again on the way home. BT was dropped off first, and for five minutes, till we got to my house, I was in the backseat alone with Mi-Su. I wanted to sneak my hand across the car seat and onto her hand. I wanted to ask her, "So, *is* he your boyfriend?" I wanted to ask her, "So, what about me?" I wanted to say all kinds of things. I wanted to scream, *"What's going on?"*

I did nothing. We sat side by side in the

dark until we came to my house. I thanked Mrs. Kelly for the ride.

I climbed out. "Bye," I said to Mi-Su.

"Bye," she said.

I shut the door. The car pulled away.

— — —

I looked down from the dormer window. Korbet Finn was riding a fish up and down the sidewalk in front of our house. The fish was orange plastic with blue wheels. A two-seater, with two sets of pedals. Korbet was in the forward seat. He pedaled furiously, back and forth, chin jutting out, churning knees boxing his chin. He didn't even glance at our house. He acted as if he had nothing else in the world to do but pedal that fish. But he wasn't fooling me. He was trying to impress my sister, hoping she was at the window, watching. Hoping she'd be so impressed that she'd burst out of the house and jump onto the backseat and go riding off with him. The pedals for the backseat went round and round by themselves, no feet to push them.

PD164

I feel like I'm playing chess in water. The pieces keep floating away. I don't know where things are. I can't figure out tomorrow.

PD165

Every day I hold my breath until I see her. Sometimes in class, sometimes in the hallway. I can't start breathing until I see her smile at me. She always does, but the next day I'm always afraid she won't. At lunch I'm afraid she'll smile more at BT than at me. I'm afraid she'll look at him in some way that she doesn't look at me. I'm afraid that when I go to bed at night I'll still be wondering. I'm always afraid. Is that what love is—fear?

Dormer-dreaming . . .

Night sky. Stars. Her whisper in my ear: "It's the Horsehead, my darling. See?" I try and try, but I can't see it. And the stars are going. All across the vastness of the universe the stars are winking out, winking out. And the empty pedals on Korbet's orange fish spin faster and faster like a runaway clock.

PD167

I sat in the auditorium today, last row, watching rehearsal. They were practicing a song about giving Iowa a try.

It was dark back there. Mi-Su couldn't see me. She looked so happy. She threw herself into it and smiled her killer smile and acted like she was facing a thousand people on Broadway. Before I snuck out, for a minute, I pretended that she knew I was there. I pretended she was performing just for me.

She tore the top off her strawberry yogurt, smacked the lunch table with the flat of her hand and said, "I'm gonna be an actress!"

"Go, girl," said BT.

"No, you're not," I said.

She stared at me. "Hello? Whose life is this?"

"You're going to be an astronomer. You said."

"That was then. Today I'm going to be an actress."

"Movies?" said BT. "Or stage?"

"Hmm." Mi-Su pressed her finger to her lips. "Stage. I love being close to my people." She stood and threw her arms out to the lunchroom mob. "My people!"

Suddenly BT was standing on the table, dancing. Mi-Su joined him. She belted out "Give Iowa a try!" All across the lunchroom kids were climbing onto tables, most of them just seizing the excuse to clown around. Yogurt cups were hopping, monitors moving . . .

PD170

I really enjoyed Monopoly last night. It was like old times, back to normal. Park Place was still Park Place. The thimble was still the thimble. BT still said "wheelin' and dealin'" and Mi-Su still couldn't stand anchovies. We just sank into the game and had fun.

PD173

I read a magazine article Mr. Bontempo sent me. It's about string theory. It says there might be another universe nearby, like one inch away from our noses, going along side by side with ours, but we'll never see it because it's in a different dimension. At the same time my mother was baking her famous Granny Smith apple pie. The smell was incredible. I sent a thought-message to the neighboring dimension: *Boy, you don't know what you're missing.*

PD175

One-month anniversary: The Kiss at Smedley Park.

No Monopoly tomorrow night. Because Mi-Su is having a party for the *Music Man* cast. Plus BT and me.

PD176

It seemed like half the school was there. When I arrived, the first thing I saw was a *Music Man* poster tacked to the front door. Inside, it was the smell of pizza and chocolate mint brownies, another dozen coming out of the oven every half hour. Cranberry punch and sodas. Get your ice cream in the kitchen and head for the dining room table to make your own sundae. Dancing in the den. Twister in the living room. *The Music Man* DVD running in the basement.

I started out hanging with BT. Most of the kids there were a grade or two ahead of me, so

I didn't know them except by name. Of course, BT didn't know them either, but he didn't care. He waded into the crowd like it was nothing. I wanted to call out to him: "Don't leave me!"

I grabbed a cup of punch and a brownie. I walked around. I tried to look comfortable. Mrs. Kelly was working the kitchen. Mi-Su was buzzing here and there, yukking it up, hugging. There was a lot of that going on: hugging. For no good reason that I could see. Show biz, I guess.

I never knew Mi-Su had so many friends. Everybody seemed so chummy-huggy with her. Packs of girls in relays headed up the stairs to her bedroom. I wanted to stand on the coffee table and announce: "Hey, people! I just think you ought to know that Mi-Su and I grew up together in this neighborhood! We've been close since grade school! She was my Valentine's date! We went to Smedley Park! We kissed! And I don't mean just a little peck either! So don't go getting all excited just because she's hugging you! Mi-Su Kelly kissed me! Twice!"

Rob Vandemeer drew a crowd. He's the star of the show. He plays Professor Harold Hill, the Music Man himself. The girls flocked around him. Mi-Su handed him a broom, and he showed everybody how he's going to strut out leading the parade. The others pumped their arms and tooted "Seventy-six Trombones." When he finished, he didn't just give the broom back to Mi-Su. He let her take the end of it, then he reeled her in till she was so close she was standing on his sneaks. Their noses were touching. Their lips puckered out like a pair of fish till they were touching, too. They broke apart, laughing. Everybody cheered (but me).

I finally found a kid I knew, a cross-country teammate, and I was talking with him at the punch bowl when I heard a familiar shriek. I looked in the living room. It was Tabby. BT was holding her upside down by her feet. She was wearing her blue cottontail bunny pj's. I looked at my watch. It was almost ten. She should have been in bed.

She saw me. She held out her arms. "Will!

Help!" BT was dunking her up and down. I didn't see my mother or father.

"What are you doing?" I said.

"I came to the party."

"Where's Mom and Dad?"

"I sneaked out."

Howls of laughter. A gaggle of girls rescued her from BT. They mauled and kissed and nuzzled her like they'd never seen a little kid before.

I heard the phone ring in the kitchen. A minute later Mrs. Kelly came out. She took Tabby from the maulers. "That was your mother, young lady. She found your bed empty and she's not too happy with you and she wants you back right this minute."

Tabby whined, "I wanna stay! Will, can I stay?"

"No," I said.

Mrs. Kelly said, "Will, you're supposed to take her home." She waggled her nose across Tabby's cheek. "You little sneak, you."

I thought: *I'm at a party, and she still finds a way to mess up my life.*

BT grabbed Tabby from Mrs. Kelly. "I'll take her home."

Mrs. Kelly said, "Wait." She pulled one of Mi-Su's jackets from the closet and wrapped it around Tabby. "You'll freeze."

BT slung Tabby over his shoulder. Tabby shrieked, "No!"

Mi-Su held the front door open, tweaked Tabby's nose as she passed. "Bye, peanut."

BT hauled his load down the walk, Tabby bellowing: "Let me stay! I'm a big kid! I can read! I wanna play Twister!"

As Tabby's voice faded, Mi-Su closed the door and suddenly the center of attention was me.

"Oh, Will! What a neat little sister!"

"She's so cute!"

"She's adorable!"

I bit my tongue and let the fuss wash over me.

When BT returned, the attention shifted to him. Girls fussed. (He was now Mr. Carried Tabby Tuppence Home.) Even guys. (Mr. Skateboarded Down Dead Man's Hill.) I was back to being Mr. Nobody. Which, really, I wouldn't have minded if only I were Mr. Somebody to Mi-Su. But it was hard to tell. I kept contriving to bump into her. A couple of times we managed to say a few words to each other, but then she would dart off to play the hostess. I started to feel like I was stalking her. Like a pest. Whatever confidence I had arrived with was totally gone. I had planned to stay after the others had left, offer to help clean up, finally get face time with Mi-Su. Now I just wanted to get out. I got my jacket from the closet. Two parades of make-believe trombones were winding through the house. They collided in the hallway. Everyone was laughing. Music was blaring. I felt conspicuous walking out the door, but no one seemed to notice.

PD178

I don't think I'll watch rehearsals anymore.

Home alone today. I took Black Viper for a spin around the neighborhood. I zipped past Mi-Su's house, forced myself not to stare as I went by. Black Viper was a whisper on the asphalt. The Stealth plane of skateboards.

Back home, I set up shop on the front step. I was installing shock pads I ordered from Fairman's. They're compressible foam, so they'll hardly raise the deck. They'll make curb jumps a little smoother and keep the wheel flanges from coming loose.

I was working the wrench when I saw Korbet heading my way.

"Hi, Will," he said.

"Korbet."

"Whatcha doing?"

"Tuning up my skateboard."

"Black Viper."

"Yeah."

"Black Viper is the coolest skateboard there ever was."

I almost chuckled. "You could say that."

"Need some help?"

"Not really."

"Can I watch?"

"Sure. Not much to see."

He sat cross-legged on the brick walkway before me. He cupped his chin in his hands, stared intensely. *Give him a thrill,* I thought. I spun the wheels. He gasped, "Wow!"

I worked. He watched.

After a while he said, "Tabby wants to ride Black Viper."

"I know."

"But she's not allowed."

"That's right."

"Never?"

"Never."

It felt like he was going to make a pitch for her, try to convince me to change my mind, but he didn't. He said, "I wish I had a skateboard."

"You will someday."

"Know what I'm going to name mine?"

"What?"

"Tabby."

"Why Tabby?" I said.

His chin bounced out of his hands. "Because she's hot!"

I bit my lip. "Yeah?"

"Yeah. And she's so pretty."

Eye of the beholder. Something mean in me—or maybe compassionate—wanted to say, Look, Korbet, she doesn't like you. Why are you wasting your time with somebody who hates your guts? What does she have to do, whack you with a baseball bat?

Then he said, "I love Tabby."

My hands stopped. I looked up. He was still staring at Black Viper. He didn't look like someone who had just announced his love. There was nothing special in his voice, just stating a fact, like apples fall down. I knew he was just a five-year-old, but I also knew he meant it, and there was nothing in this disappearing world that my sister and a hundred baseball bats could do about it.

"That so?" I said.

He nodded. "Yeah."

"Don't you like any other girls?"

He shook his head. "Nope."

I fit the front shock pad over the screws. Korbet's tongue showed at the side of his mouth. He was staring so hard I could almost hear his eyes squeak.

152

"Start first grade next year?" I said.

His head bobbed up. "Yeah. I hope I get the same teacher as Tabby." He stared some more, then said, "Will?"

"Yeah?"

"You think we'll get the same teacher? Me and Tabby?"

"Maybe," I said. Come on, make the kid feel good. "Probably."

His face lit up. "Yeah!"

More staring, then: "Will?"

"Yeah?"

"I wish you were my big brother."

Wow. I knew I didn't deserve it. "Thanks, Korbet."

"Then Tabby would be my sister and then she would *have* to like me."

Oops. OK, let it lie. Let him believe it. Don't say: Got news for you, kid—it doesn't always work that way. She doesn't even like me.

I said nothing.

"Will?"

"Korbet."

"If you were my big brother, you could walk me down the aisle."

He meant the aisle in the auditorium at

Roosevelt Elementary. Years ago somebody decided that we're always celebrating endings (graduations) and never the beginning. So now there's a ceremony each September for all the little kids about to enter first grade. It's called First Day. Each little kid walks down the aisle to the stage holding the hand of a big kid. The ideal is for the big kid to be a brother or sister who's in twelfth grade. But any big kid will do. Sibling. Cousin. Friend. Parents and grandparents get all weepy. I guess I'll have to go down the aisle with my sister, but I'm not exactly looking forward to it.

"Somebody will walk you down, Korbet," I said. "Don't worry."

Neither of us spoke for a while. The shock pad was snug. I was tightening the last of the nuts when he said, "I love you, Will."

Where did that *come from? What do I say? "I love you, too, Korbet"? "Back at ya, Korbet"? "Thanks, Korbet"?* I stared at the wrench, blinking. Time passed. And then it hit me: he didn't need an answer. Probably didn't expect one. I swung my eyes from the wrench to his face, and I saw I was right. I smiled. He smiled.

Suddenly I wanted to talk.

"Korbet?"

His eyes fixed on mine. "Huh?"

"Korbet . . . you don't think Tabby likes you back, do you?"

He wagged his head wildly. "No way!"

"But you still like her."

"Yep."

"Do you think she'll ever start liking you?"

"Yep."

"When?"

He thought about it, dug into his ear, looked at the sky, looked at me. "Next year."

I bit my lip.

"Do you think about her a lot?"

He beamed. "Yeah. Lots!"

"When you're playing?"

"Yeah!"

"When you're eating?"

"Yeah!"

"When you're washing your feet?"

"Yeah!"

He doubled over laughing.

"So, Korbet . . . are you ever, like, timid around her?"

"What's timid?"

"Never mind. What about scared?"

He looked puzzled. "Huh?"

"Are you ever scared of her?"

He mulled that for a moment, then laughed. "Hey, Will, you're funnin' me. Tabby's not scary."

"Yeah, just funnin'," I said. "But, you know, like, sometimes she's not real nice to you? Like she hollers at you or shuts the door in your face?"

"Yeah?"

"So . . . how's that make you feel?"

He was puzzled again. "What do you mean, Will?"

"Does it make you sad? Upset?"

He thought hard. He said, "It makes me sad for two seconds. Then I love her again."

Double wow.

"And when you think of her playing with other little boys, do you get jealous?"

Korbet's eyes slid past me, focused on something else. He smiled hugely, waved.

There was a beep behind me. Our car pulled into the driveway. Mom, Dad and Tabby spilled out.

"Hi, Korbet," said my mom.

"Hi, Korbet," said my dad. He tousled Korbet's hair as he went by.

"Hi, Tabby," said Korbet. Tabby said nothing. She didn't even look at him. She shot him her tongue out of the side of her mouth and scooted on past him and into the house.

I looked at Korbet. He didn't seem devastated. Those two seconds had already passed. He said, "What's jealous?"

PD187

Mi-Su is nice to me. She smiles at me all the time. Such a nice smile. She's nice to me in algebra. She's nice to me in Spanish. She's nice to me in English. She's nice in the hallways and the lunchroom and before school and after school and on the weekends and Saturday-night Monopoly. Nice. Nice. Nice. I

hate nice. So what *do* I want? I don't know.
But I don't want nice.

PD191

plink
   plink
   plink

What?
I opened my eyes. Smooth, brown, plastic
surface. My wastebasket. Sitting by my pillow.
Tabby. Grinning. Dropping black jelly beans.
One by one. Into the basket.
   plink
I moved. She ran screaming from my
room. The basket toppled to the floor. Clatter!
Jelly beans rolled under the bed. Dad called,
"What's going on?" Tabby screamed, "Mischief
Night!"
It wasn't night, and it definitely wasn't
Mischief Night, which around here is the night
before Halloween, which is seven months

from now. But ever since Tabby heard about Mischief Night, and ever since she was told that she would not be allowed to go out like a big kid and terrorize the neighborhood, she's been threatening to have her own Mischief Night.

I was slowly waking up. In front of my face my left wrist was coming into focus—it was naked! My atomic watch was gone! I sleep with it. She must have snuck in and weaseled it off my wrist. I went ballistic. I roared into her room. I dragged her out from under her bed. The watch was too big for her wrist. It was on her ankle. I yanked it off. I said something murderous. She squealed, "Mischief Night!"

Evidence of other crimes today:

- a string of Elmer's Glue on the toilet seats
- a vacuum cleaner humming inside the dining room closet
- four sinks, a shower, two bathtubs, a laundry room tub—every faucet in the house running
- a pile of Lucky Charms on the living room rug

- the doorbell is ringing—nobody's there (a hundred times)

At least my trophy was safe, hidden away for the day. Ditto Black Viper.

BT came to the rescue, took her outside for skateboard lessons. "Don't leave the driveway," Mom told them. Crazy as BT is with himself, he's never that way with Tabby. He never lets her roll off the driveway.

I watched them from the dormer window. If you drove by and saw them, you'd think they're brother and sister. I thought of BT's little sister bringing her hurt knee to him, laughing when he fixed it. . . .

▬ ▬ ▬

BT stayed for dinner. He was in the kitchen helping my mother with the rigatoni. Tabby was on the phone with Aunt Nancy. Well, not really—she just punched the number, yelled "Mischief Night!" into the phone and hung up. When she turned she found me standing there. She screamed, "BT!" and tried to run. I held her. From the look on her face, she thought this was it, the Big Counterattack. She thinks that someday I'm going to get so fed up with her tormenting me that I'm going to blow my stack and come after her with all guns blazing. She flailed. "BT! BT!" All I wanted to do was ask her something, but the violence of her struggle surprised me, the terror in her eyes. I let her go. She bolted like a freed animal.

At dinner she wanted to sit on BT's lap. My father wouldn't let her. She pouted.

I asked her, in front of everybody, "Why don't you like Korbet?"

Shock showed on the faces of my parents and BT, like: *Whoa, Will just spoke to Tabby!* They all turned to her.

Tabby was cutting her spaghetti into pieces with her blue plastic saw. She stabbed a meatball with her screwdriver. She held it up to her mouth and licked at the sauce, like it was a Popsicle. She took a bite out of the meatball, chewed with her mouth open, grinned meatball mush. I finally realized she had no intention of answering my question. For once in my life I give her some attention and she hangs me out to dry. I wanted to plead Korbet's case, tell her what a great little kid he is, but it wasn't going to happen.

All my mother said to Tabby was, "Chew with your mouth shut."

PD194

Another week of nice from Mi-Su. I'm sick of nice.

PD200

Two hundred days since 10:15 A.M. that September Saturday morning when Riley picked his nose and the phone rang and Mi-Su said turn on 98.5 FM and I learned that a proton had died in Yellowknife. How many have died since then across the universe? Are dying protons like roaches: for every one you see there's a hundred behind the wall? How many

need to die before it starts to show? Before
steel becomes transparent? And people? Ghost
world. I feel a twitch. A blip. Was that a tiny
flash inside of me? Is my liver down one proton from yesterday?

HERE LIES WILL TUPPENCE
(OR WHAT'S LEFT OF HIM)

PD201

Idea!
eBay!
Nice be gone!

PD208

It came today, my order from eBay. It's a little figurine not much bigger than the pewter
king on my chess trophy. It's a band member.
Tall red and white feathered hat. Red and

gold jacket. White pants. Playing a trombone. A tiny gold-gilt trombone. A label on the bottom says "76 TROMBONES." It's from *The Music Man*!

It's plastic. It's cheap. I don't care. I'm thrilled.

PD209

How shall I do it? All I know for sure is how not to do it. Don't give it to her at school. Don't give it to her at Saturday-night Monopoly. Think . . . think . . .

PD210

Thinking . . .

PD211

Got it!

PD213

I wrapped it up. White paper, red bow. One word on the tag: "Mi-Su." Skateboarded over to her house yesterday. Sunday. Walked the last block. Had to be careful she wasn't outside. Snuck up to the front step, laid it down on the bricks, rang the bell, ran, hid on the far side of the garage. I was hoping she would answer the door. She usually does, runs for it like a little kid. But even if one of her parents answered, I could live with that. I peeked around the corner.

She opened the door. Frowned. Looked around. Looked down. Picked it up. Tore it open right there. Squealed. Came out farther. Looked up and down the street. Called to the empty street, "Hey? . . . Hello?" Looked again at the figurine. Kissed it. Held it up in the sunlight, the tiny trombone gleaming. "Thank you!"

I stepped out. "You're welcome."

She turned, saw me, came running, threw her arms around my neck, kissed me, squealed, "Where did you *get* it?"

"Oh, somewhere," I said, mucho cool.

We spent the rest of the day together. If she touched me once, she touched me a hundred times. Big, long, non-nice kiss good-night.

Today I'm floating through school. She blew me a kiss in the hallway. Is there a Cloud Ten?

PD214

Up in the dormer before dinner. Staring at her roof. Imagining her in her house, moving from room to room, humming *Music Man* tunes. The show will be Friday and Saturday nights.

At lunch today she said to BT and me, "So, which night are you guys coming?"

"Friday, of course," said BT. "Saturday's

Monopoly." He deadpanned at her. "You're not giving up Monopoly to do that stupid play, are you?"

She looked at him, her face blank for a half second, then caught the twinkle in his eye and broke out laughing.

I said, "Both."

She turned to me. "Huh?"

"I'm going both nights."

I'm not sure they believed me.

I was tempted to ask her to the dance right there. The freshman dance is next month. I've been thinking of it since Valentine's night. I probably would have asked her already, but I held off because things were uncertain there for a while. Now I'm ready to roll. Or at least, ready to plan. Valentine's night and the *Music Man* figurine worked out well. So I know that's the way to go for the dance.

In fact, the plan is already in place. It just came to me. I guess I'm getting good at this. I'm going to do it this Saturday night, right after the last performance of the play. I'll meet her in the lobby, or maybe even backstage. She'll be flushed and breathless and glowing from excitement, and I'll congratulate her and we'll hug and then I'll say something like, "Well, y'know, just because the play is over doesn't mean you have to stop dancing. Let's go to the freshman dance together." And she'll squeal out "I'd love to!" or "Yes!" or whatever and we'll hug again and so forth.

I can see it so clearly. After three or four days of this, I'll hardly be able to tell it from a memory, it will be so real. In fact, the looking forward will be so much fun that when Saturday finally comes, I'll probably wish I had another week to think about it. I'll carry my thoughts around with me like soda in a cup, sipping through a straw whenever I feel like a taste: during class, on my skateboard, lying down to sleep, especially then.

I'm that way, goofy as it sounds. Sometimes I don't want things to happen—I'm talking about good things, even wonderful things— because once they happen, I can't look forward to them anymore. But there's an upside, too. Once a wonderful thing is over, I'm not all that sad because then I can start thinking about it, reliving and reliving it in the virtual world in my head.

Down below, BT was giving Tabby skate-board lessons in the driveway. She was arguing with him about something. The word "Now!" kept coming up through the window-pane. If I had to pick one word to sum up her life, I guess that would be it:

HERE LIES TABITHA TUPPENCE
NOW!

PD215

Sipping . . . sipping . . .

PD216

Mrs. Mi-Su Tuppence
　Mrs. Mi-Su Tuppence
　Mrs. Mi-Su Tuppence

The play was great. And totally different from the rehearsals I've seen. The bright stage lights. Every seat filled. Suddenly I had a new perspective on Mi-Su and her fellow actors. I knew why I'd never try out for a school play. And I knew Mi-Su and the others were nervous; she told me so. But that didn't stop them. They were talking and dancing and singing as if they were actually enjoying themselves. As if they were all going down their own Dead Man's Hill.

The play was great again. Standing ovation.

I waited in the lobby with all the parents, grandparents, etc. She came out laughing with others, stage makeup still on her face, her eyes bigger than ever, dazzling, like, Doesn't anybody want to take my picture? Her parents beamed, held out their arms. "My baby star!"

her mother cried. I didn't want to be too pushy. Give her time with her family, cast members.

Finally she noticed me. For a split second she didn't react, and I had the weirdest feeling she didn't know who I was, but then came the famous smile and I went to her and held out my arms like her parents and we hugged and I whispered in her ear, "You were sensational," and she whispered back, "Thank you."

That's when it occurred to me that I had a problem. The lobby was crowded with people. No privacy. If she went right home, it would probably be in her parents' car. Meanwhile, other cast members were saying they should all go out and celebrate, that's what show biz people do after the last performance. So when, where, how was I going to ask her to the dance?

I considered waiting till tomorrow, Sunday, but all week long I'd been locked into the plan. Time was coming to a point. I tugged on her sleeve. "C'mere a sec." I led her a couple of steps away. We were standing in front of the trophy case. Bright lights. Chattering, laughing people. I tried to remember my words.

"Your singing was great," I said.

She chuckled. "You couldn't hear me." Her eyes were flying.

"Sure, I could," I said. "And your dancing was great, too." I was starting to feel stupid. She just looked at me, waiting, wondering. "So . . . ," I said, and jumped in, "Let's go to the freshman dance." She just stared at me. "OK?"

She said, "You mean together?" The smile was still there, but it wasn't real.

I felt a chill. "Yeah. 'Course."

Her eyes wouldn't look at me. Her smile tilted. "I was afraid you were going to ask me."

Afraid? *Afraid?*

"What do you mean?" I said.

"Somebody already asked me."

My kneecaps fell to my feet. I thought: BT!

"Who?" I said. And thought: *No, not BT.* I remembered the cast party at her house, and I knew. The star of the party. Star of the show. Mr. Music Man himself. Rob Vandemeer.

"Danny Riggs."

I thought I heard her say Danny Riggs.

"Huh?" I said.

"Danny Riggs."

She *did* say Danny Riggs.

"Who's Danny Riggs?"

She shrugged. "A guy."

This was all so strange. I felt like I'd stumbled into the wrong conversation. Or into one of those string theory parallel dimensions.

I said, "What kinda guy?"

She laughed. "A guy kinda guy. He's on the stage crew. He makes scenery."

"He asked you?"

She laughed again. "Is that so shocking?" She struck a pose. "I'm cute. I'm a star. Who wouldn't want to ask me?"

All I could say was, "When?"

The smile vanished. "Last week. Nobody else"—finally her eyes swung into mine—"*nobody else* was asking, soooo . . ."

I just stared at her. And at the trophy case, at a tall silver quartet of Greek columns and a blue stone plate that said:

BASKETBALL CHAMPIONS
DISTRICT ONE
1998

I felt her hand on my arm. "Hey, no big deal." The smile was back. She looked around. "Gotta go. See ya." And she was gone.

I turned to the bright lights, the bright, chattering, laughing people. I wondered if one of them was Danny Riggs.

PD219

In the dormer. Staring at her roof.

Warm. Window open. Along the street forsythias hurled yellow fountains. In the driveway below, BT and Tabby were fighting. She wanted to skateboard on the sidewalk. He wouldn't let her.

Danny Riggs . . . Danny Riggs . . . I couldn't get the name out of my head. I was sad. I was mad. I was jealous. Sadmadjealous. Still couldn't believe it. How could some other guy know her well enough to ask her to the dance and me not even know about him? I racked my brain, trying to remember her ever saying his name before. Who did he think he was? Didn't he know we grew up together? That we were like brother and sister for years until we started to notice each other another way? Didn't he know that his dance date, the dazzling Miss Mi-Su Kelly, kissed me—me!—on Valentine's night? And again just last Sunday, only one short week ago?

Down below BT was showing off, doing stunts for Tabby. They're called ollies. Tabby tried to do an olly, fell. They laughed.

I wandered through the dormer. What were we saving all this stuff for? A framed painting of a seashore landscape leaned against the stationary bicycle. I ran my finger along the top edge. My fingertip was gray. Dust. Everything was dusty except my telescope and the wedding gifts.

I ran a silver ribbon between my fingers. I tugged slightly. It held firm. Still tightly tied after all these years. The silver paper was fading to white along some edges and corners, where the afternoon sun strikes. Seventy-eight years they've been sitting, waiting. A hundred years from now will they still be here, the wedding gifts of Margaret and Andrew Tuppence, waiting, unopened?

Nightmare. I'm being chased by a swarm of fireflies.

Danny Riggs. Danny Riggs.

I spent the day checking.

He just moved here last year. He lives on Hastings, right behind the school. Homeroom 113. I got out two minutes early, rushed to 113, waited in the hallway. He's taller than me. Skinny. Blond crew cut. Braces. Earring. Cheap clothes. Wal-Mart. Payless.

I followed him. Easy to do in the after-school mob. Pretty soon we were the only two. I hung way back, wondered where he was going, wondered why he was walking so far, no skateboard. Terror: *he's heading for Mi-Su's!* He wasn't. When we got downtown he went into Snips. Maybe his mother is a hair-dresser.

After dinner I took Black Viper for a cruise past her house. About ten times. I wanted her to come out. I didn't want her to come out. Was she behind a window, seeing me, purposely not coming out? What would I say if she did?

She didn't.

I hate Danny Riggs.

I hate BT. This all started when he kissed Mi-Su at the star party last October.

I wanted to talk to Korbet. Suddenly talking to Korbet Finn was the thing I wanted most in the world. I pushed off, raced home, rang his bell. Mrs. Finn answered, smiled. "Will." Or more like, "*Will?*" Because, even though they're right alongside us, I never show up at their door. And here I was, a teenage big kid coming to ask for their five-year-old, like, "Can Korbet come out to play?" I had to think fast.

"Hi, Mrs. Finn. Can I see Korbet a second? I have this paper to do in school and I need to talk to a little kid."

"Well," she said, "he turns down most interviews, but let me see." I just stood there with a dumb cow face; I was too preoccupied to realize she was being funny. "Come on in."

"Uh, this would work better outside," I said. Stupid.

When he appeared in front of me in the doorway beaming and said, "Hi, Will!" I was so happy I wanted to cry. We sat on my front step. I asked him a couple of stupid questions just in case his mother interrogated him. He took it all in stride. He didn't seem to notice or care that a teenager had showed up asking for him. Now that I had him here, I didn't know what to say.

His lips were blue. "Been eating blueberry water ice?" I asked him.

"Smackin' Jacks," he said. "Want one?" He was ready to run and get me one.

I told him no thanks.

I couldn't help staring at him. This little survivor. He took incredible abuse from Tabby and still kept coming back. No visible scars, no limp in his personality. Going with the flow. How did he do it? Was it his age, or did he have something I didn't have?

He picked a blade of grass, stuck it up his nose.

"Ever hear of protons?" I said.

An April ant moved across the flagstone at his feet. He placed the blade of grass in front of it. It walked around. "What're protons?"

"They're little," I said.

He brightened. "Like ants?"

"Smaller," I said.

He thought. He looked around. He grinned. "A cootie?"

"Smaller."

He wasn't sure whether to laugh or not. He knocked my knee. "You're funnin' me, Will. Nothing's littler than a cootie."

"You could fit a billion protons into the eyeball of a flea," I told him.

His mouth dropped. His eyes went wide. He knew from my face and my voice that I wasn't kidding, he knew it must be true, but it wouldn't stick to his brain. I wanted to say, Korbet, I'm sad. Can you make me feel better?

I said, "Protons die."

He looked at me. "Do they go to Heaven?"

How could I answer that? "Korbet," I said, "what would you do if you liked a girl—"

He jumped in, beaming. "I *do*! Tabby! I *love* her!"

"—I know—if you liked a girl and you asked her to go to a dance with you but somebody else already asked her first? What would you do?"

He uncurled his index finger, propped his chin on it. He pondered grimly for half a minute, staring off down the street. At last he nodded. He looked up. The gray of his eyes matched the flagstone. He looked older than five. He spoke: "Ask her to the *next* dance."

PD221

I've been playing a lot of chess with my father. The tournament is this coming Saturday. Every once in a while it occurs to me that I'm defending champion. I used to practice all the time. I should have been gearing up for weeks, but I haven't. I can't concentrate. My father beat me yesterday. I stunk.

Today was no better. It felt like all I did was stare at my father's defense. Did I want to sacrifice my queen to open up the board? Or take the safe route and capture his knight? My eyes kept drifting to the back row, to his king and queen. But that's not what I saw. Instead of the royal couple, I saw Mi-Su and Danny Riggs, dancing in a black-and-white checkerboard ballroom.

"Daddy! Come here, quick!"

Tabby was at the door. Dad and I were locked in my parents' bedroom. It's our Tabby defense. She knows chess takes concentration, so she tries to disrupt us whenever she gets wind that we're playing. She always calls out for my father, but of course it's me and my concentration she's really after. Sometimes I'm amazed at how devious a five-year-old can be.

"Daddy!"

My father ignored her. He once told me that he allows her to do it because it's good training for me—I must be able to shut out distractions.

"Daddy!"

"I can't think," I said.

"Focus," he whispered.

Except for the pest, we tried to simulate tournament conditions. A timer sat on the table.

"Daddy! There's something in the hallway! Come quick!"

The king and queen were waltzing across the floor . . . time was running out . . . couldn't think . . . couldn't think . . . blindly I moved my rook, took his knight. I hardly had time to pop my clock before Dad pounced, sending his bishop clear across the board, into my king's face. "Check," he said.

Never saw it coming. Now I was in big trouble.

"Daddy! Mommy wants you!"

My turn again. It was no disgrace to lose to my father. It happens half the time. But I never get trounced, and today he was trouncing me. I could tell he was disappointed in me. But I also knew he wouldn't let up. Even when I was little, he never let me win. When I finally did, I knew I'd earned it. He groomed me for that tournament. When I won, he was so proud. And now I was letting him down. Somewhere Mi-Su and Danny Riggs were smiling dreamily at each other and my sister was pounding on the door and I couldn't think . . . couldn't think . . . the clock was ticking . . .

"Daddy! I'm bleeding!"

Ticking . . .

I roared: "Tabby! Shut up!"

My father's eyes flared.

The clock pinged.

I was out of time. I couldn't believe it. That hadn't happened to me since I was six. My father was staring at me. I couldn't read his face.

"It's her fault," I said.

My father was moving pieces, resetting them for another game. But something was wrong—when I told Tabby to shut up, she shut up. For the last minute, nothing but silence from the other side of the bedroom door. And now I heard a faint sound. A kind of hissing, sipping sound. I turned in my chair. A red and white striped straw was poking under the door. She'd done this before. She was trying to force us to come out by sucking the air out of the room. When I turned back, my father's neck was red. He was biting his lip.

We were first at the lunch table. Alone for the moment, if you can call being in the same room with three hundred other students alone. We had both brought our lunches from home. We unwrapped our sandwiches. I felt her staring.

"Hi, Grumpy," she said.

I looked up. She was smiling sweetly. "Huh?"

"I said, 'Hi, Grumpy.'"

I looked around. "You talking to me?"

"No, I'm talking to your chicken salad sandwich."

"Who's Grumpy?" I said.

"You."

"Me?"

"Yeah, you. Grumpy. Sourpuss. All week."

I smiled. "I'm not grumpy."

She laughed. "*That* . . . is the fakiest smile I've ever seen in my whole life."

"Fakiest isn't a word," I told her.

She was silent for a while; then: "Will."

"What?"

"Will."

"What?"

"Look at me."

I looked at her.

"Will . . . it's just a dance. He asked me first. We're only in ninth grade. There's three more years. No big deal. I still like you. Get over it."

BT and others were heading our way. I shrugged. "I'm over it."

PD223

I lost again to my father yesterday. And on my way to losing today. I'm going to lose in the first round on Saturday. I'm not only going to lose, I'm going to be embarrassed. I'll be exposed as a fake and a fraud and a fluke. People will say, "He's no good. Last year's win was a fluke." They'll make me give my trophy back. "You're a disgrace to the tournament," they'll say. I don't want to go. I hope I get sick. I'm losing and I'm sad and I'm grumpy and the rooks and pawns keep looking up at me, like,

"So what's the next move, dummy?"and I'm *not* over it and Tabby was pounding on the door . . . pounding on the door . . .

I punched my clock button.

My father looked up. "You didn't move."

"I'm not going," I told him.

He cocked his head. "Not going? Not going where?"

"To the tournament. Saturday. I'm not ready, and I can't *get* ready because of her. Maybe you can focus with all that racket, but I can't. I'm not you. I'm not going."

My father yelled past me, "Tabby! Stop!"

My father hardly ever raises his voice. When he does, Tabby hides in her bedroom closet. I heard her running off.

My father restarted the timer.

I punched it.

"I'm not going," I repeated. "It's too late. She's ruined a week of practice."

"She's gone," he said. "She won't be back."

"It's not just that," I said. "She'll be there all day Saturday. She's into my head now. Just knowing she's there in the audience—" I knew I was reaching but I didn't care; I'd unleashed my mouth and it was taking off. "I'm hearing her in my dreams. I'll be stinko. I'll make a fool of myself."

He stared at me. I met his eyes. Did he believe me? His shoulders went up and down as he took a deep breath and let it out. Was he giving up on me? My son, the quitter? He nodded. "Hang in there. We'll see. Give yourself the rest of the night off. Watch some TV. Clear your head." He got up and unlocked the door.

PD224

My father hasn't said a word about tomorrow. Is he letting me off the hook? At least there's one thing I can control: Mi-Su and BT. They cheered me on last time. This morning at school I told them both I wasn't entering the tournament this year, so don't bother showing up. Of course they wanted to know why. I was going to make up some fancy lie, but then I had a brilliant idea: tell the truth (or at least part of it). So I told them my sister was driving me crazy and I couldn't get any quality practice time in and I didn't want to embarrass myself in front of my best friends and so I wasn't going. They believed it.

In the afternoon I came around a corner and bumped smack into Danny Riggs. He said, "Hi, Will," and we went our ways. My name coming out of his mouth—why did it shock me? Why am I surprised he even knows it? He gave a little smile with it. Was he being the gracious victor? Being nice to the poor pathetic loser, the *former* boyfriend?

I'm aching for the old days, before the star party and the kisses and the complications, before the tiny flying flashes, when we were all just friends and the biggest problem on Saturday nights was how many hotels to build on Park Place.

PD225

My pillow was warm with sun when my father poked his head into my room. "Let's go, champ. Up and at 'em."

Until that moment I wasn't sure I was going. I still didn't want to. I had hoped he would let me sleep, but I guess I knew better.

By the time I got down to breakfast, Tabby was wagging her head and saying, "No . . . no . . ." Her mouth was full of dry Lucky Charms.

"Don't you want to be with Aunt Nancy?" said my mother.

"I hate Aunt Nancy."

"Stop being silly. You'll have a good time."

"I want my ice cream."

"There's ice cream in the fridge. Rocky Road. Just for you."

"I'm going to Purple Cow. I want my banana split."

"We'll take you to Purple Cow next week."

She pounded the table. She spewed Lucky Charms. "No! Today! I go to the termament!"

I was getting the picture. My parents had told her she was staying home, to be babysat by Aunt Nancy. For the last two years they've brought her with them to the tournament. It takes place in the gym at Lionville Middle

School. There's not much for little kids to do but sit and watch from morning till night. She kept getting itchy. Once, she ran down from the bleachers and snuck up behind me and put her hands over my eyes and said, "Guess who?" When the monitor came after her, she ran screaming like a banshee around the players' tables. Another time she stood up in the bleachers and belted out: "Go, Will! Beat his pants off!"

That's when my mother dragged her off and took her to the nearby Purple Cow and told her she could get anything she wanted. She got the deluxe super-duper banana split. It took her over an hour to eat. For the last couple of weeks my mother has been telling her that if she's good at the tournament, they'll go to Purple Cow for another banana split. That's really why Tabby wanted to go to Lionville, not to see me play chess. And Aunt Nancy couldn't take her to Purple Cow because Aunt Nancy doesn't drive.

Tabby dumped her bowl of milkless Lucky Charms onto the kitchen table. She stood on her chair. She stomped her foot. "I'm going!"

My father took her by the upper arms and lowered her to the floor. He kept hold of her as he sat on the chair and brought his face down to hers. "You have lots of days. You get your way a lot. This is Will's day. You're not going." He said it calmly, softly. She jerked away from him and ran upstairs bawling. But not before giving me a look, a look that said, *Will's day, huh? So you're the one behind all this.*

■ ■ ■

Actually, it's not exactly true that Aunt Nancy doesn't drive. She does drive a bicycle. She pulled into the driveway at 7:30, and a minute later the three of us were on our way to Lionville.

My first opponent was a girl named Renee from Great Valley. Much to my surprise, I beat her. In only ten moves. Then I beat a guy from Conestoga High, a senior. I called checkmate before his king had time to straighten his crown.

I was on a roll, and I didn't know why. Maybe my father was right, taking time off cleared my head. Maybe my sister's shenanigans distracted me from Mi-Su and Danny Riggs. All I know is, the more I won the more I wanted to win. Sixty-four kids had started the tournament. Two quick games—twenty-two moves—and already I was in the Sweet Sixteen. I began to picture a second trophy standing alongside the first.

We went out for lunch break, to Purple Cow. Back in the gym, I zipped through my first match of the afternoon. That put me in the quarterfinals. Three rounds to paydirt. I was thinking: *Cakewalk*. Then, finally, I met some competition, a huge blobby crew-cut freckled red-haired junior from Henderson. Even his fat arms had freckles. And tattoos. Whales. Swimming in a sea of freckles. He called himself Orca. Not exactly your chessy type. But as soon as he rejected my queen's gambit, I knew he was trouble.

Five moves. Ten moves. Twenty. Thirty. Moves and countermoves. We were neck and neck. The board was smoking. You are truly focused when you're so focused that you don't know you're focused. I wasn't seeing trophies. I wasn't seeing the crowd. I wasn't seeing

Orca. I wasn't even seeing pawns and rooks and bishops. I was seeing the board. The whole board. Everything. That's the key, to see it all, to see the patterns, the pitfalls, the possibilities. To blinder your brain until you're in the zone, until your whole universe is the eighteen-by-eighteen-inch checkered chessboard in front of you.

Me: Rook to bishop, one.

Orca: Pawn to bishop, three.

Me: Bishop to queen, three.

My hope here was to lure Orca into moving his pawn to queen's knight, three. It's a trap Dad often sets for me.

Orca: Pawn to queen's knight, three.

Yes!

I pinched my pawn. With it I would take his pawn. By itself, an innocent little move, but it would be the beginning of the end. He was doomed, and he knew it. He was on the gangplank, and every move of mine from now on would be a sword tip poking him farther and farther out until—*Checkmate!*—he became shark meat.

I was about to lift my pawn when I felt a

hand on my shoulder. But even then I stayed with it, stayed in the zone, my eighteen-by-eighteen-inch world.

"Will—"

My father's voice.

"Not now," I said.

The hand squeezed. "Will." I turned my head, looked up. His face wasn't right. "We have to go."

"I can't," I said. I didn't know why he was doing this, but I was sure he was kidding. Or testing me.

"Come on," he said. His voice was husky.

"I'm winning," I said. I might have whined. "Four more moves and I'm in the semis." Orca was staring, mouth open.

My father pulled my chair out as if I weighed nothing. He pulled me to my feet and led me off the floor. The gym was silent except for our footsteps. Only now, with my dad yanking me out of my zone, did I realize how much fun I had been having. I couldn't remember the last time chess had been fun.

My mother was waiting in the hallway. She was crying. She reached out and took my hand. I didn't know she could squeeze so hard. "Tabby's hurt," she said.

All I could come up with was one brilliant word: "What?" She was already heading out the door.

My father talked as he drove to the hospital. Aunt Nancy said the morning had gone normally, Tabby watching her Saturday cartoons. They had hot dogs for lunch. About an hour later Aunt Nancy went upstairs to check on Tabby. The TV was on in her room, but no Tabby. Aunt Nancy looked around the house—dormer, basement, everywhere. Called for her. Nothing. She went outside. Korbet was playing in his backyard. No, he hadn't seen Tabby. Neither had his parents.

Aunt Nancy walked up and down the street, calling. She got on her bike and rode around the block. She rode in bigger and bigger circles around the house. She was all the way out to Heather Lane when she heard an ambulance siren. People were standing at the top of Dead Man's Hill.

"Little girl—" they said.

"Skateboard—"

"Crashed—"

"Trauma center—"

Aunt Nancy wouldn't know a cell phone from a muskrat. She raced back, called my folks from the house.

— — —

We passed the first carnival of the year, at the Greek Orthodox church. Tilt-A-Whirl looked like an alien spaceship gone berserk. A sign said "Souvlaki! Folk Dancing!" At the hospital all the closest parking spaces were for doctors. My father cursed them and parked in the last row. Halfway across the lot my mother gave a little squeak and broke into a run. In all my life I had never seen her run. My father started running, too. Then me.

Emergency smelled like mouthwash. There were no rooms, just spaces divided by white curtains. Behind a counter a nurse looked up. She seemed surprised to see us. "Yes?"

"Tabby Tuppence," said my father.

"Oh yes." She pencil-pointed to one of the spaces. It was mobbed with white-coated people. You couldn't even see the bed. "Right there. But we'll have to ask you—"

My mother was already marching. The nurse called, "Ma'am!" like my mother was really going to stop. At the bed my mother stood on tiptoes and looked over the white shoulders. Then a man nurse led her away, and we all went to sit in a little room with a TV and old magazines and a man and lady in the corner. The lady was sniffling. The man had his hand on her knee. He had the biggest ears I'd ever seen.

We sat. Waited. Read year-old health and gardening magazines. After forever, a white-coated man came in. He smiled and looked down at us. "Mr. and Mrs. Tuppence?"

A mangled syllable fell out of my father's mouth.

"I'm Dr. Fryman."

I thought: *No, you're not. You're Dr. Short.* Because he was so short. Not a dwarf, but not a heck of a lot taller either.

He held out his hand for shaking. When he came to me, he said, "And you are?"

"Will," I said. I was surprised at the strength

of his tiny hand. It felt funny looking down at a doctor.

He nodded, smiled, finally let go of my hand. "She's in intensive care now. You'll be able to see her." He held out his arm. "But why don't we go in here first."

He led us into another small room, this one empty. The seats had cushions. There was a stained-glass window in the back wall.

"Sit. Please," he said.

We sat. He sat. When he sat he wasn't much shorter than when he stood.

"Tabby?" he said. "Short for"—his eyebrows went up—"Tabitha?"

My mother's breath caught on a snag. "Yes."

The doctor smiled. I wondered why he was smiling so much. A hearing aid was molded into one of his ears. It looked like someone had pressed bubblegum in there.

"Well, she had quite a spill there," he said.

"Will she be OK?" my mother blurted.

He looked at her, smiled. "We hope so. We believe so."

A pen top peeked out of his white coat

pocket. It was a yellow smiley face.

"She's had some lacerations, here and there. We did some sutures, in her scalp, her knees. You'll see some bruising. She may have had a concussion, so we'll keep an eye on that. Mostly we're concerned with her neck area."

My mother gasped. My father croaked, "What?"

"Well, general trauma. There may have been some damage to the windpipe. Or"—big smile, friendly shrug—"there may not have been. We'll be testing. Time will tell. Meanwhile, she was having a little trouble breathing—"

A hiccuppy sound from my mother. *"Breathing?"*

"A *little*?" said my father.

"—so we've got her intubated now."

"What's intubated?" I heard myself say.

"We've inserted a tube into her trachea—that's the windpipe—and a ventilator is breathing for her."

"Breathing *for* her?" my mother squeaked.

The doctor reached over and touched the back of my mother's hand with his fingertips.

He looked around. He got up and came back with a thin black and gold book that said *Prayers*. The inside of the back cover was blank. He took out the smiley face pen and drew a picture. "This is the trachea . . . bronchial passages . . . lungs. The tube goes in here—"

"Up her *nose*?" Me again.

"Oh, sure," he said, like no big deal. "Works best that way."

I was remembering one morning when I woke up with her sitting on my chest and saying, "I'm a walwus." Carrot sticks stuck out of her nose. She tried to clamp her laugh, but it came out as a snort and the carrots speared me in the face.

My father was asking a question: " . . . need a ventilator to breathe for her?"

The doctor clipped the pen back in his pocket. He closed the book. "We do it all the time, Mr. Tuppence. In Tabby's case, it's to let things calm down in there. Give things a rest. Let the machine do the work."

He made it sound so natural, like the machine was Tabby II. I wanted to see this machine.

My mother stood. "Can we see her now?"

The rest of us stood. We looked down at the doctor. He smiled. "Of course. Just one more thing"—the room stopped breathing—"we've got her sedated. As I said, we want things to calm down. We don't want her getting upset, trying to pull the tube out, you know? So we'll keep her asleep for a while."

"How long is a while?" said my father.

"That'll be up to Tabby, how she comes along. Not a minute more than necessary."

My father's hands flew out. Suddenly his voice was loud and clear. "A *week*? A *year*?" He trotted after my mother, who had already taken off. "*Ten* years?" He was almost shouting.

When I got to the corridor I didn't see my parents, but I did see the letters "ICU" on a glass door. *Intensive care unit*, I thought brilliantly. I pushed a button to open the door, and there I was. There were real walls here, but no fronts. Cubicles. In an arc fanning out from the nurses' station. You could see every bed. No mob of white coats. No parents. They must have missed the sign.

"Tabby Tuppence?" I said to the nurse behind the counter.

She finished writing something, looked up. "You are?"

"Will Tuppence."

She smiled. "Brother?"

I nodded. This was getting so stupid it wasn't worth wasting a word on.

"Number three." She nodded, toward number three, I assumed, but as I walked across the floor I couldn't see a number three, or any other number, anywhere. I stopped. I thought, *Jeez, can't anybody put up number signs in this place?* I took my best guess on which cubicle was number three. Sure enough, there was a little kid in the bed, and there was a tube up her nose. Or his nose. I couldn't tell. The face was all swollen and blue and his/her head was covered with a bowl of bandages. Whatever, it wasn't Tabby, which was a relief. But this was getting ridiculous. I didn't have all day. I went back to the nurse.

"I'm looking for Tabby Tuppence," I said. "She's supposed to be in number three."

The nurse looked confused, like I was

talking rocket science or something. "I believe"—she looked at the clipboard she was carrying—"she is."

I pointed to the cubicle. "Is that number three?"

"Yes," she said.

"Well, she's not there."

More wide-eyed confusion. I had always thought hospitals were pretty competent places. "She's *not*?"

"No. That's not her. I know my sister." I said it slow: "Ta-bi-tha Tup-pence."

At that point the nurse headed for the cubicle and my parents finally showed up. "Mom," I said, "they're all messed up." I threw my hands out. "They can't even get numbers right around here."

The nurse's voice came from the cubicle. "Sir . . . this *is* Tabitha Tuppence."

I'd had enough. I pointed at the nurse, shouted, "No, it's not!"

And suddenly my mother had me in her arms, squeezing me, and over her shoulder I saw my father standing at the bed, looking down, and I knew.

— — —

It was dark when we walked out of the hospital, my father and me. My mother stayed behind. They said she could use a nearby room, but she said she would stay in number three.

On the way home I wondered if Orca had gone on to win the tournament after I forfeited to him. The carnival was still, dark, deserted. Empty Ferris wheel seats dangled against the night.

As we pulled into the driveway, the head-lights caught Aunt Nancy's bike sprawled in the grass and Mi-Su and BT sitting on the front step. Mi-Su came running, her face lopsided from crying. She hugged my father. "How is she?"

"Sleeping," he said.

She peered into the car. "Where's Mrs. Tuppence?"

"Staying."

Mi-Su gave a shudder, and then she was hugging me. She squeezed as hard as my mother. Then BT hugging me. I can't remember us ever hugging before. I'm not a huggy kind of guy. My father asked them to come in, but they said no thanks and left.

Aunt Nancy was sitting on the sofa. Black Viper lay on its back in her lap. She looked up at my father. Her face was blotchy. She dabbed at her eyes with a Kleenex. "How is she?"

My father was taking a long time to answer, so I said, "She's fine."

I took Black Viper from her lap. I spun a wheel—smooth as ever. Shock pad tight. On top a little chipped paint, that was all. Almost good as new.

Aunt Nancy gave me a piece of paper. "Found it under the door." I unfolded it. It was in green crayon, all jumbo letters until he nearly ran out of space for his name:

DEER TABBY
GET WELL SOON I
LOVE YOO
KORBET

My father tied Aunt Nancy's bike into the trunk and drove her home. I went to bed. I didn't even bother to take my shoes off. Did I sleep? Did I dream? I don't know. I only know in the middle of the night as I lay there I was aware of a presence in the dormer, of something happening there. I got up. I stood at the foot of the stairs. I saw—I imagined—who knows?—fluttering lights beneath the dormer door. And I knew what it was. Time itself had gone into hyperdrive. All was accelerating. Protons were swarming in the dormer, swarming and flashing out of existence by the billions, lighting up the wedding gifts. And somehow I knew that if I walked up those stairs and opened the door and went in, I'd never come back down again.

I went downstairs, got the skateboard, went outside. I dropped the skateboard to the ground, stepped on, pushed off, stopped. "No!" I said to the night. I shoved it with my foot. It wobbled across the lawn to the sidewalk. I picked it up, whirled it like a discus thrower, let go. It sailed into the house, just missing the front picture window, dropped into a bush. I could hear the wheels spinning.

I walked the streets. My atomic watch glowed green in the dark. It told me the time.

It told me the month, day and year. It didn't tell me what was going to happen to my sister. I walked, walked. I could no longer see the whole board, only my own dark square.

PD226

The phone rang. I staggered from bed.

"'Lo?"

"You're sleeping. I'm sorry."

Mi-Su.

"'Time is it?"

"Almost eleven. I didn't really expect anyone to be home. Just thought I'd try."

I spied a note under my door. "Wait."

I picked up the note. It said:

I wanted to let you sleep. I'll be at the hospital.
Dad

I returned to the phone. "I went to bed late," I told her. "I was out."

"Out?"

"Walking." Silence. "Hello?"

"I'll let you sleep."

"No. Wait."

More silence. Then: "What am I waiting for?"

I tried to think. "I don't know."

She gave a half-giggle. "Well, I was just calling to see if there was any news, that's all. I'll check later."

"I'm up now. I'm not going back to bed."

"You want me to come over? I have two muffins here."

"OK."

— — —

The muffins were cranberry. I don't like cranberries, but it didn't matter because I couldn't taste the muffin anyway. She had made us herbal tea she found in the cupboard. This I could taste. It was like flowers.

"So where did you walk last night?" she said.

"Nowhere special. Just around."

"She'll be OK."

"I know."

We picked at our muffins, a crumb at a time.

"I hate cranberries," I said.

"Pick them out. Give them to me."

I picked out the cranberries, dropped them on her plate.

"I hate this tea."

"It's good for you."

We chewed. Sipped. Sat.

She started to say something. "What time—"

"It's all BT's fault," I said.

Her eyes came up, brows arching. "Really?"

"He got her started on the skateboard. They're always in the driveway."

"His fault."

"Not just that. His craziness, too. Doing crazy stuff. Stunts. She sees it. She wants to be like him."

"You think so?" She was grinning, I didn't know why.

"She thinks he's great."

"Don't you?"

"I think he's going to end up pumping gas."

The grin grew. "I think you love him."

"That's a weird thing to say."

"What are you doing?"

The grin was gone. She was staring at the table. I looked. My hand was a fist. It was mashing the cranberry muffin into the plate.

"Will—"

"It's my fault."

"No." I was surprised how fast the "No" came, as if she had been waiting for me to say that.

I nodded. "Oh, yeah. It is."

She lifted my fist from the mashed muffin, swept away the sticking crumbs with her napkin. "No. It is not your fault."

"She was making noise when I was playing chess with my dad. Bothering me"—I looked at her—"you know?"

She nodded. Her eyes were shining.

"So I told my dad I wasn't going to the tournament if she went. Take your choice— her or me—I told him. So she . . . she didn't go. They told her yesterday morning, 'You're not going.' She went ballistic. Not because of the chess."

Mi-Su rasped, "Ice cream."

"Yeah. Exactly. Ice cream. She couldn't care less about my chess. And the thing is . . . the thing is . . ."

Her hand came over, rested on mine. "What's the thing?"

" . . . thing is . . . how she looked at me . . . she knew . . ."

"Knew what?"

"Taking Black Viper. Going down Dead Man's Hill, like BT. She knew exactly what to do to get back at me."

Mi-Su wagged her head wearily. She pushed herself up from her chair and walked slowly upstairs. I followed. She stopped at the doorway to Tabby's room. "I just wanted to see . . . ," she said. Her voice caught. "Oh . . . poor Ozzie. All alone." Ozzie the octopus was flopped forlornly over Tabby's pillow.

When Mi-Su turned to me, her face was glary. "You're so . . . It's not about chess or ice cream or skateboards or BT or anything else. It's about you. You and her. She loves you. That's all it's about. She *loves* you, you stupid . . . idiot . . . brother."

She went downstairs. I heard the front door open, then her calling: "And *you* love her!" The door closed.

I went into her room. Sat on the bed, looking at Ozzie. If I could draw sadness, I'd draw that plush gray toy octopus. I petted its soccer ball–size head and left the room.

— — —

As I left the house a little later, I nearly tripped over BT. He was sitting on the front step.

"Why didn't you come in?" I said. "The door was open."

He shrugged. He didn't get up.

"Mi-Su was here."

He nodded. "I saw her."

Out of habit, I glanced around for Black Viper, then remembered last night. Only the black tip was showing above the bush, as if it was drowning. "I'm going back to the hospital."

He nodded.

I headed for the sidewalk.

"I'm sorry," he said.

I stopped, turned. "What about?"

His face was down, his elbows on his knees. "I never should've gone down the Hill. It gave her the idea." He was crying.

I came back to him. "That's bull." I said. "It's not your fault."

"I taught her to skateboard. She copied everything I did. I should have known she would try that."

It didn't feel right, standing above my life-long friend, looking down on the top of his head. "No, no. She copied you at a lot of good stuff. She thinks, like, you're *it*, man. Don't you know that? She thinks you can do no wrong."

He gave a sneering sob. "Yeah, that's the problem."

I put my hand on his shoulder. Before I could take it away his hand was squeezing mine.

"BT, listen," I said, "there's nothing for you to feel bad about. You've been like another"—the word wanted to stay put but I shoved it out—"brother to her."

And thought: *The brother I haven't been.*

I extracted my hand. If I didn't get out of there right then, I was going to lose it. I gave him a little arm punch. "She loves you. Gotta go." I trotted off.

— — —

Back in intensive care, seeing her, I couldn't stop a cockeyed thought: *mummy*. With the bandage bowl over her head and all the tape across her face holding the tube tight to her nose. And what little I could see of her face was purple. Crazy as it sounds, about twenty-five percent of me still didn't believe it was really her. It wouldn't have surprised me one bit if the doctor had come in and said, "Sorry, folks, there's been a mistake. This isn't Tabitha."

More tape held needles in her arms. More tubes ran from the needles up to plastic bags hanging above her. The bags held liquid. One was clear as water. The other looked like flat ginger ale. Tubes up her nose, in her mouth.

She looked so tiny in the bed, like they couldn't find one to fit her. The ventilator was a high-tech–looking contraption with little lights and all. If somebody had told me it was the latest thing in home entertainment, I'd probably have believed it—until I heard the sound it makes. Kind of like breathing. Wheezing. But not human breathing. Not little five-year-old girl breathing. Machine breathing. Alien breathing.

"What's that?" I asked my mother and father. I was pointing to a sky-blue plastic clip on the end of her index finger. Reminded me of a clothespin. A light in the clip made her fingertip glow red, like ET.

"It measures oxygen in the blood," said my mother.

"Pulse oximeter," said Dad.

My mother looked terrible, like she just got out of bed. "Doctor say anything?" I asked her.

She took a deep breath. "About the same. Her vital signs are good."

"What's that?" I said.

Dad said, "Blood pressure. Pulse rate. Respiration"—he looked at the wheezing ventilator—"well—" We all looked at the ventilator. Respiration means breathing. The ventilator was breathing. My sister was not breathing. So the ventilator's vital signs were good. Hurrah for the ventilator.

The tiny doctor came in. Smiled. Shook my hand. Said, "Good morning, Will." *It's afternoon, you moron,* I thought but didn't say. He put his stethoscope on Tabby's chest. *Why don't you put it on the ventilator?* He glanced at the blinking lights, the little green numbers. Felt the tubes. Said some medical jibby jabby to my parents. Said, "MRI good . . . X-ray good . . . blood work good . . ." *If everything's so good, what the hell's she doing here?*

When the doctor left, my mother said, "Did you eat?"

"Yeah," I said. "Mi-Su came over."

"I could use something." She got up. "Why don't you come with me?"

We walked through a maze to a crowded cafeteria. My mother got an apple juice and a plain bagel. "Here," she said, leading me outside. We wound up in a courtyard, a little square secret surrounded by the building. There were orange and yellow daffodils and a tree gushing dark pink blossoms. Pink petals covered the ground. There was a wooden bench with iron curlicue armrests. We sat.

She ripped the bagel, offered me a piece.

"No thanks," I said.

She sighed, chewed, sipped apple juice.

"Dad says you were sleeping when he left."

"Yeah."

"Snoring."

"I don't snore."

"He says you were." Why would my father say that? "He says you were out walking last night."

"Yeah."

"How are you feeling?"

"Great."

She took my hand, squeezed my fingers. "I hate to see you worried, but in a way I'm glad you are."

"Why wouldn't I be?"

"I don't mean it that way. I knew you would be." Her voice sagged, like her shoulders. "I just know how pestered you feel sometimes."

"*Some* times?" I tried to say it with a grin.

She laughed, squeezed my fingers. "I know . . . I know . . ." She stared at me, looked away—"Will"—looked back at me— "Will . . . why do you think she throws her black jelly beans in the wastebasket?"

"She knows they're my favorite."

"And?"

"To tick me off."

"And?"

I shrugged. "What else is there? It's like everything else. She makes sure I see her, because if I don't see her I won't get mad. And that's what she wants, to make me mad."

My mother closed her eyes and gave a weary sigh. "You're hopeless." She hugged me as she said it. "Did you come on your skateboard?"

"No."

She looked surprised, then not surprised. "I need you to go home and meet me back here."

"I still have legs."

She squeezed my knee. "Good. An hour time enough?"

"Yeah," I said. "Easy."

"Okay. When you get there, go to your sister's room and take a look at Ozzie. A really close look. Then come back and tell me what you find." She pushed me from the seat. "Go. I'll meet you right here in an hour."

Home was less than a cross-country course

away. I was there in twenty minutes. I took the stairs two at a time. Ozzie looked pretty normal to me, until I turned him over and saw the gash in his underside that was laced up like a sneaker. I untied the laces and pulled it open and reached inside and pulled out a Morningside lemonade container. A mailing label said in big red letters:

FOR WILL—TOP SECRET!!!

The words looked adult-made, but I figured I knew who did the dictating. I took off the yellow plastic lid. The container was three-quarters full—of black jelly beans.

I don't know how long I sat there, staring at the jelly beans, at the gutted octopus. The horizontal world I had thought I occupied was tilting, dumping me somewhere else, somewhere new. I carefully replaced the container in the octopus and returned to the hospital.

■ ■ ■

I waited on the bench. When Mom sat beside me, she stared at my face for a long time. At last she said, "You found it?"

I nodded.

"And?" Still searching my face.

"And . . ." I shrugged. I had feelings but not words.

She laid her hand on mine. "Let me get you started. You're not exactly sure what to make of Tabby's little secret, but you think you just saw a side of her that you maybe hadn't noticed before. Does that come close?"

I nodded.

She looked away with a long sigh. "Do you know what she does afterward, when you're *not* looking?"

I shook my head.

"She takes the jelly beans back out of the wastebasket. She dusts them off. She has her own special dust rag. Then she puts them in her secret place. She's going to give them to you on your next birthday."

"Dusted off?" The words came out choky.

She squeezed my hand. "Don't worry. She won't know it, but I'll substitute new jelly beans at the last minute."

I didn't know what to do, what to say.

Feelings were flooding. I reached up, flicked at the end of a gushing pink branch. Petals fell.

I felt her head on my shoulder. "Will . . . she's too little to understand the best way to get you to love her. So she just does it her way."

Something in me wouldn't give up. "Which is being a pest." But this time I smiled as I said it.

She poked my knee. "Exactly. Why do you think she keeps fooling with your trophy? Because she thinks you love that little pewter man more than her." Her breath caught on the last word. "Sometimes you"—she made a fist and punched my knee twice, thumb out, girl-style—"you get so wrapped up in your own little world you don't see what's right in front of you. Whatever interests you—*you*—that's what she zeroes in on."

Chess
Trophy
Skateboard
Black jelly beans
Star party
Mi-Su
BT

I cleared my throat. "There's something I always wondered about."

"What's that?"

"The wedding gifts. Why hasn't she ever ripped them open?"

She nodded, gave a quiet chuckle. "I threatened her. I told her if she ever messed with the gifts, you would not walk down the aisle with her on First Day."

We sat for a while, breathing.

Now she was lightly rubbing my knee, brushing away the punches. "You know what she wants? More than anything?" I shook my head. "She wants to be just like you. Her big brother."

She hugged my arm. "Do you even know what color her eyes are, Will? Do you?"

Petals falling . . . pink petals falling everywhere . . .

I don't know how my mother stands it, staying in the room all this time. Every other minute she checks the tubes, reads the monitors. She touches Tabby's face. She reaches under the sheet to feel if her feet are cold. She holds her hand, runs her finger over it, kisses it. She rubs her earlobes between her thumb and forefinger. I've never seen earlobes get so much attention.

She talks to Tabby as if she can hear. She says things like, "Will's here," and "Mommy's going to go see the nurse. I'll be right back," and "Korbet says hello." She reads Korbet's note to her. I'm not sure if this is a good idea, knowing how Tabby feels about Korbet, but I don't say anything. She reads picture books to her. My father has brought a stack from home. *The Velveteen Rabbit*, *Chicken Little*, etc. I think of BT reading adult murder mysteries to her. She would prefer that.

The doctor calls it an "induced coma." Keeping her "asleep on purpose"—that's how he said it. "Asleep on purpose." So "things can settle down." He comes in. The nurses come in. "So far, so good," everybody says.

I want to believe it. I want to believe she's just sleeping. But I don't. I don't know where she is, but it's not sleep. And I don't believe this "so far, so good" crap either. Neither do my parents, I can tell. The tiny doctor says they'll stop the medicine—I think it's dripping from one of those bags—little by little, and they'll turn off the ventilator and she'll wake up, and then they'll really know how she's doing. My mother said, "When?" The tiny doctor said, "As soon as possible." I wanted to club him.

I had to get out. Move.

I ran through neighborhoods, other lives, other worlds. Solipsism. A man on his lawn mower. Green and yellow. A high-school kid with earphones, washing his car, suds creeping down the driveway. High in the bright blue sky the moon showed like a fading fingerprint. It seemed so weak, so out of place, as if it stumbled into broad daylight by mistake. Unseen protons dying by the billions.

My footfalls came down like periods to my mother's words:

She wants to be just like you.
She wants to be just like you.
She wants to be just like you.

— — —

Like a riderless horse, I wound up back at my house. Another look at the room, at Ozzie, smiling at the thought of the hidden jelly beans. I stood at the top of the stairs and said, in the empty house: "My sister loves me."

Light blinking: phone message: Mi-Su: "Hi. Just checking. Wish I were family, so I could come. I called Danny. I told him I couldn't go to the dance. Not with Tabby . . . so . . . well . . . just letting you know. Bye."

— — —

I returned to the hospital to find that Dad had finally persuaded Mom to go home for a little while, just to get a shower, change clothes. She whispered in Tabby's ear. "I'll be back in an hour, sweetie. Not a minute longer. Daddy's going to drive me home. Will's here. Maybe he'll read to you. He loves you." She kissed her ear, said to me, "Back in an hour. You're OK?"

"Yeah," I said.

"Sure?"

"Mom. Go."

They went.

We were alone.

The ventilator wheezed. The hanging bags dripped. The little green numbers told her vital signs. Under PULSE the number was 65. Her fingertip glowed red. Oximeter. I remembered the time I woke up with her straddling my chest, saying "Wally ate a potato every day." I wanted to go back to that moment right then.

I pulled the chair close, till it was touching the bed. For the first time I noticed the other plastic bag, hanging from the side of the bed. I guessed what it was: yet another tube in her, so she can pee. I don't know why, but just thinking of this, seeing how her pee filled up half the bag, made me really happy, like, "She's working!"

I was afraid to touch her. Her face was so purple and swollen, like her cheeks were stuffed with socks. Where the tube entered her nose, the transparent plastic was foggy. I touched her little finger, just touched it. Then I held her hand, the one that didn't glow. I was thinking of when sometimes—crossing a street or parking lot—my mother or father tells her to hold my hand and, boy, does she love that. And she milks it. She comes up and she doesn't just slip her hand into mine so we can get this over with as quickly and painlessly as possible. Oh no. She jabs her hand up—she'd wave it in my face if she were tall enough—and gives me her snooty grin and says, "Mommy says you *hafta* hold my hand." She sneers the last three words. So I snatch her hand and off we go . . . and now, thinking back on it, remembering how furious I would get, I was a little surprised that I've never given her just a little retaliation squeeze, a little finger-masher. The second we hit the other side of the street—it never fails—she yanks her hand from mine and cheats me out of the satisfaction of being the one to let go, and away she runs yelping like a banshee.

She wasn't squeezing now. Her hand just flumped, limp as one of Ozzie's eight arms.

The sheet moved faintly—up, down, up, down—to the rhythm of the ventilator. I touched her chest—three fingertips lightly—up, down, up, down . . .

Maybe he'll read to you.

I took the top book from the stack. *Silly Goose.* I started reading. I stopped. Geese? Chickens? Rabbits? She didn't want to hear this stuff. "Hold on," I said. "Don't go anywhere."

I ran to the patient library down the hall and was back in five minutes with a ratty copy of *The Murderous Maid.* I began to read aloud: "When Harold Jensen looked out the window he saw a sky-blue Chevrolet pull up to the curb. An attractive woman, her red hair tied up in a bun, got out of the car. She put on a pair of glasses and stared directly at his front door. She referred to a piece of paper in her hand. *Probably making sure she has the right address,* thought Harold. 'Dear,' he called to his wife in the kitchen, 'I think the person you're interviewing for the job has arrived.'"

I tried to read with expression, but there

was no reaction from Tabby. By the end of the first chapter the story was heating up pretty good. I was about to begin chapter two when I remembered my mother's question. I laid the book down. I took a deep breath, felt creepy. *Just do it.* I reached down to her bruised and swollen face. My hand trembled. I placed the tip of my finger on her closed eyelid. *Is this possible? Only one way to find out.* I slid my fingertip down till I felt her feathery eyelashes. I applied a slight pressure. I held my breath. I pushed upward. The eyelid came up, like a tiny shutter, a shade. Her eye stared at me. *She sees me. She sees me not.* It was green. A bold green that surprised me. A green I'd seen before but couldn't remember where.

— — —

At home in the kitchen I found a lopsided cake with chocolate icing and two handmade notes to Tabby from the chipmunks. I'd bet four hotels on Park Place that BT made the cake himself.

— — —

In the night I dreamed:

I'm underground. Buried alive. Can't see. Can't breathe. Can't move. My fingernails claw at the dirt. Above me—a sound. It's BT, sweeping the metal detector, looking for me. I hear the hum of the detector coming closer . . . closer . . . I claw, try to scream "I'm here!" but my mouth only fills with dirt and the humming gets louder and louder and suddenly it's not BT anymore, it's Tabby, and she's singing "Wally ate a potato every day" over and over and I'm trying to scream . . . trying to scream . . .

PD228

My father didn't go to work. My mother slept in the hospital again last night. My father woke me up, said, "School today." So next thing I knew I was sitting in algebra class. Wondering why.

Mi-Su was in the next aisle, two seats up, working her pencil, crossing stuff out. Every few minutes I remembered that she cancelled the dance with Danny Riggs. A week ago I would have been jumping for joy.

Whenever she looked at me her eyes were sad. Afraid. I told her, "Don't worry. She'll be all right."

Kids kept saying things:

"Oh Will . . ."

"How's your sister?"

"Hey man, I heard . . ."

Once, I heard a whisper behind me: "Dead Man's Hill!"

The period ended. I grabbed my books and walked out of the classroom and . . . out of the school.

Outside!

Heading for the street.

Did I really leave school in the middle of the day?

I think I pulled a BT.

■ ■ ■

In the house. Alone. So quiet. Empty. Not right.

I zombied from room to room. I sat on the

edge of her bed. It's little-kid size, not like the ICU bed. No tubes, no ventilators, just bed. Just room. Sad-sack Ozzie on the pillow. Witch's broomstick in the corner. She begged for it for Christmas. When she doesn't sleep with Ozzie, she sleeps with the broomstick. On the floor, her toolbox. And a paperback novel, from her personal librarian, BT. *The Magpie Murders.*

Also on the floor, a coloring book. *Let's Be Bears.* I picked it up, paged through it. She gets colors all wrong. Green sky. Blue bears. Even at her age I made my skies blue. There has never been a time when I didn't know the sky is blue, the grass is green, bears are brown.

I heard something outside. I went to the window. It was Korbet. He must have been staying home from kindergarten today. He pedaled his orange fish back and forth in front of our house. He pedaled furiously, hunched over. Back and forth . . . back and forth . . .

It was like he was trying to make her well. He figured if he pedaled hard enough, long enough, she would be OK, she'd come home.

I drifted around the house. Empty.

Helpless. I wished there were an orange fish I could pedal furiously.

I heard her voice in distant rooms . . .

Where's the party?

In yer dreams, lugnut!

Daddy! I'm bleeding!

I'm a big kid!

Mischief Night!

Bob, you smell bad.

I stood in the kitchen, and it was that September Saturday morning again. The smell of strawberries. Tabby saying, "Riley picked his nose." Tabby answering the phone. Tabby saying, "Phooey!" Tabby jabbing the phone in my face: "For *yyew*." Mi-Su: "Quick!" The voice on the radio. The proton dead. Tabby . . . Tabby dropping slices of sweet potato in the toaster . . . Tabby climbing onto the counter . . .

I sat on the counter. I said the words:

"Riley—"

"Picked—"

"His—"

"Nose!"

And jumped to the floor. Dishes rattled.

It was all I could think of to do. Since she couldn't be her, I'd be her.

I got my own secret stash of black jelly beans from my bedroom closet. I dropped them into a wastebasket one by one:

plink

plink

plink

I yelled, "Mischief Night!"

I dumped a pile of Lucky Charms onto the living room carpet.

I let the vacuum cleaner run in the closet.

I turned on every faucet in the house.

The phone rang. I picked it up—"Barney's Saloon"—and slammed it back down.

I went to my room, turned my trophy around.

The phone rang. I picked it up—"Barney's Saloon"—slammed it back down.

I went up to the dormer. I stood before the wedding gifts. I closed my eyes. I saw her in the ICU, so small in the bed, the tubes, the bags, the contraptions . . . I tore open a gift. Silvery wrappings, silver ribbons flew. Downstairs the phone was ringing. I tore open more gifts. Here were towels, thin little towels, lacy borders. A blue teakettle, white speckles, tin, I think. Two glasses, stemmed, tulip shaped. A wooden tray, little carved angels facing each other from the handle holes. A set of wooden salad bowls. A pillow, with red and blue stitching: "Home, Sweet Home." Picture albums, black pages. A fancy, brassy mantle clock.

In one of the boxes, an envelope. It said "Betsy." Not Margaret. All my life I've known my great-grandmother as Margaret. But it wasn't. It was Betsy. They called her Betsy. She called herself Betsy. And that made all the difference. I ran to the telescope. Crazy, I know, but . . . why not? I looked through the eyepiece, turned the focus knob . . . yes . . . there . . . 1930 . . . I saw them, Betsy and Andrew Tuppence, dashing down to the pier, the huge ship foghorning *Hurry! Hurry!* Her shoes in her hands, wedding dress flashing white, a swan taking off, Andrew calling *"Wait!"* the two of them laughing . . . laughing . . . all the way to Africa . . .

———

I went downstairs, passed the ringing phone, picked up—"Phooey!"—slammed down, went outside. Korbet was pedaling in slow motion now, exhausted. Tear tracks stained his cheeks. He looked at me as if I could fix things. I turned away.

There was really only one place left to go, one thing left to do. I pulled Black Viper out of the bush. I didn't ride it, I carried it by one wheel. The streets were deserted—of people, not flowers. Lots of flowers. A pretty, people-less day in May.

For the second time in the past year I stood at the top of Dead Man's Hill, one foot on Black Viper, one on the ground. It had been hard to imagine BT standing here, ready to go down. It was impossible to imagine Tabby. Was she thinking: *I hate Will. He made me miss my ice cream.* Was she thinking: *I'll show 'em all.* Was she thinking: *Mischief Night!*

I looked over the town. I could see my neighborhood, my roof. Mi-Su's was blocked by trees. There was BT's house. Smedley Park. The clock tower on the Brimley Building. Still couldn't make out the time from there. I wondered if they'd ever fix it, or would BT's little stunt last forever? Were the lives of the townspeople changing in slight, unnoticed ways because the clock that looms over them every day is wrong? I looked at the watch strapped to my wrist, the second hand perfectly ticking off the seconds of my life, the dying of protons, the slow, silent, unfeelable passing of the cosmos, and suddenly I knew exactly what Tabby had been thinking. She was thinking: *I'm scared*. The world blurred. Tears poured. God! She was scared to death. She was shaking. And *still* she did it. She's so little she can't even tell time, and she did it, she pushed off . . . I could hear her screaming, and Black Viper couldn't hold, Black Viper was flying . . . and I felt her foot on the board next to mine, her brave little foot holding, holding, and her voice came whispering: . . . *see me . . . see me . . .*

I kicked Black Viper down the hill and walked away.

— — —

"Where *were* you?"

My mother marched across the ICU, met me at the nurses' station. She was mad.

"Around," I said.

"We called you at school, at home."

I felt a chill. I looked over her shoulder. Tabby was still in the bed, my father staring down at her. But something was different.

I looked at my mother. "They're bringing her out of it," she said. "We wanted you to be here."

"What do you mean?"

"She's waking up."

"She's OK?"

"We don't know yet. They do it gradually. The doctor says so far, so good."

"That's what he always says."

She nodded, chuckled. She hugged me. She whispered, "She spoke. Her eyes were closed but she said something."

I was afraid to ask. "What?"

Her voice trembled in my ear: "See me . . ."

I was drowning in white light.

"Afternoon, Will," said the tiny doctor. His white coat fell almost to his shoes. "No school today?"

"Not for me."

He touched my arm. He was fooling with ventilator settings. "She's almost weaned off now. She seems to be breathing fine on her own, but we'll keep the ventilator handy just in case. Sedation is very light now."

"So far so good," I said.

"Exactly."

The doctor checked a drip bag and walked out.

My mother sat on the edge of the bed. She took Tabby's hand. She brought it to her lips, kissed it. I sat beside her. She gave me a faint smile. She placed Tabby's hand in mine. She moved so I could slide closer. My sister's hand was so small in mine. I wiggled each of her fingers. I looked at her face, her eyes. I bent down. Her ear was so small. I whispered, "I love you, Tabby." There was no movement of her eyes, no flutter of eyelids, no twitch of the lips. I knelt at the bedside. I whispered. "I tore open the wedding gifts. Beat you to it. Don't tell Mom. And guess what? They called great-grandmom Betsy." I told her everything. I told her I'd take her to Purple Cow for ice cream. I told her I threw Black Viper away but I'll buy her her own skateboard and she can ride it anytime she wants as long as I'm there and it's not down Dead Man's Hill. I told her we'll go to star parties and I'll take a thermos of hot chocolate and she can have half. I'll sneak her a cup of coffee. I told her Mi-Su and BT said hello. I even put in a good word for Korbet. I went on and on, and her eyes were still and, thinking back, I don't know when it started, but all of a sudden I was aware of my hand, and I looked, and her fingers were curled around my thumb and they were squeezing.

SEPTEMBER 2

FIRST DAY

Roosevelt Elementary. Lobby. It's a madhouse.
I haven't been in here since I graduated.
Folding chairs have been set up, the gym has
become an auditorium, and the parents are
out there in their seats, waiting for their little
darlings to come marching in.

Every kid about to start first grade tomor-
row is here, and every one of them is jabbering.
I can't believe what a big deal this is to them.
Was I this excited when I passed the pebble?
That's what they call it: Passing the Pebble. I still
have mine. It's the size of a marble, painted

blue. My mother kept it these past ten years. She gave it to me this morning. You might have thought she was giving me a diamond. It's OK if you've lost your blue pebble; the principal hovering around here will give you one. But it's best if you still have yours from your own First Day, because the idea is to pass the pebble from one generation to the next. You walk down the aisle with your new first grader, there's a ceremony on stage, and then the big finale when the high schoolers pass the pebbles to the first graders and everybody goes bonkers and the mothers cry.

Tabby jabbers, jabbers. To look at her, to listen to her, you'd never guess where she was four months ago. Once she came to, there was no shutting her up. The doctor made a joke: "Would you like me to put her back under again?" Today she wears something I've hardly ever seen her in: a dress. It's green. It doesn't quite match her eyes. Only one thing does. It finally came to me about a month ago. I was in the dormer when I smelled it drifting up two flights of stairs: pie. And suddenly I knew where I had seen her eye color before, in the kitchen, my mother slicing Granny Smith apples. And the sweet apple oven cloud carried the only poem that's ever visited me:

> *Imagine my surprise—*
> *She's got Granny apple eyes!*

She jabbers at all the other firsties. She jabbers at Mi-Su, who will walk Korbet down the aisle. And—glory be!—she even jabbers at Korbet, and you can see the kid is in Heaven. She jabbers at BT, who will be the only high schooler taking two kids, his twin sisters, the chipmunks. For once they're almost still. Tabby doesn't say a word to me. She doesn't have to. Through all the jabbering she's got her hand wrapped around my finger. Even though it's not time yet. She hasn't let go since we left the house.

I peek into the auditorium. My parents and Aunt Nancy are out there somewhere. My mother surprised me with her reaction to the wedding gift disaster—she didn't seem to care. In fact, the torn paper and ribbons and open boxes are still in a heap as I left them. At least, that's what I'm told, because I myself haven't been up in the dormer since Tabby came home from the hospital. Mom says she'll get around to cleaning up the mess someday. Or maybe not. She says Betsy and Andrew were probably waiting for someone to come along and rip open the gifts for them.

Mi-Su, BT and I stand here like giants, grinning at each other over this sea of little heads. Tabby's jabber stitches us together. We say nothing to each other. We don't need to. During Tabby's recovery, Mi-Su and BT were at our house every day. They mostly ignored me. BT promised to take Tabby with him next time he does something crazy. And Mi-Su— every Friday throughout the summer she showed up with her toothbrush and at nine o'clock crawled into bed with Tabby for the night.

It was the best summer of my life.

Then last Saturday night a miracle happened. Maybe two. The three of us were having our usual Monopoly and pizza binge. BT bought his usual railroads, but somehow he also wound up owning two hotels on Park

244

Place. And guess where I landed? Rent: three thousand bucks. Wiped me out. For some reason I found that really funny. As I went to fork over the money, Mi-Su stayed my hand. Her eyebrows went up, her grin went impy: "I could give you a loan."

I stared at her, at BT. Echoes of all my no-loans-to-BT speeches filled the room. I burst out laughing. We all did.

When we finally calmed down, Mi-Su said, "You finally did it."

"Did what?"

"You laughed out loud."

I thought about it. "I guess I did, huh?"

"You did, dude," said BT.

"You're becoming positively impulsive," said Mi-Su.

"Yeah?"

"Oh, yeah."

I feel closer than ever to BT and Mi-Su. Or maybe close isn't the word—maybe it's comfortable. I'm OK now with BT and his ways. Not that I'm ready to climb clock towers with him, but I don't see him as an exotic creature in a zoo anymore. I don't measure him against myself. He is who he is, and—president or gas-pumper—he will be who he will be. I wouldn't want him any other way.

As for Mi-Su and me, well, I don't know exactly where we're heading. And I don't care. I don't need to know anymore. I don't need to know who we're going to be tomorrow or next year or ten years from now. It's enough to know who we are today, this minute, and who we are right now are two good friends, as good as friends get, smiling at each other across the jabbering little heads and not giving a rat's lugnut that the world is vanishing one proton at a time.

■ ■ ■

Music is coming over the PA. Kermit the Frog singing *The Rainbow Connection*. The principal goes, "Shhh!" but the jabbering has already stopped. Little hands grope for big hands. We line up alphabetically according to the firsties' last names. BT and the twins are toward the front. Then Mi-Su and Korbet. Tabby and I are near the end.

Korbet looks back, panicked. Finally his

eyes land on Tabby. They thumbs-up each other, he turns back, pulls Mi-Su into the auditorium, pumps his fist in the air. The audience is standing, turning toward the aisle. We're moving. We've been told to give each first grader plenty of room, don't crowd the ones in front of us—they're the stars. *The Rainbow Connection* recycles. Couple by couple—big kid–little kid, big kid–little kid—the mob is draining from the lobby.

And now it's us.

We stand at the doorway. I feel the pebble in my pocket. I wait until the two before us are halfway down the aisle. I look down at Tabby. She's staring straight up at me, serious, waiting. "Ready?" I say. She nods sharply. "Ready." We step into the brighter lights of the auditorium. We're walking down the aisle . . . faces are smiling . . . faces are smiling and Kermit the Frog is singing and the clock on the Brimley tower is now three hours behind and I haven't seen a tiny flash in months and Tabby wears a Granny apple dress and a Granny apple ribbon in her hair and shoes and socks of the purest white I've ever seen and she's squeezing my finger like there's no tomorrow and she's here and she's now and so am I and that's all there is and I'm walking down the aisle with my sister . . .

. . . and I'm walking down the aisle with my sister . . .

. . . and I'm walking down the aisle with my sister . . .

. . . and I'm walking down the aisle with my sister . . .

Smiles to Go

EXTRAS

A Letter from Jerry Spinelli

Dear Reader,

One thing is for sure if you become a published author—you'll be asked, "Do you have any advice for someone who wants to become a writer?" I'm no exception, and my answer is always the same: Write what you *care* about. Over the years I've known for certain only one person who's taken my advice: me. I did it with *Maniac Magee* and with *Stargirl* and with *Milkweed* and with most of my other books. And now I've done it with *Smiles to Go*.

When the book was ready to come out, the publisher sent me on a tour of bookstores. Since I was going to be talking directly to people about my book, I had to come up with things to say about it—brief, meaningful, sound-bite things. As I tried to summarize the story in a couple of words, the two I kept coming up with were *time* and *love*. So there I am being asked what my book is about and I say, "It's about time and love." Doesn't exactly knock your freckles off, does it? Those two words are as big and vague as fog. There's nothing to sink your teeth into, not a detail in sight.

And yet, to this day I haven't been able to come up with a better concise description of the book.

3

Because, foggy or not, that's exactly what *Smiles to Go* is about: time and love. All of which goes to show, I guess, that it's better to read the book than the sound bite. What I hope I've done is dress up those two foggy notions with color and detail and tension and drama. I've wrung a *story* out of those two words, a story that I hope you find interesting.

It's a story that takes the biggest things of all (eternity, the cosmos) and the smallest things of all (atoms, subatomic particles), the most magical things of all (wonder at nature's grandeur, a kiss under falling stars) and the most ordinary (the smell of strawberries, a pesty little sister)—it takes these disparate things and mixes them into a story. A story that begins with a proton and ends with a smile. A story that I care about—see, I take my own advice—and that I hope you will care about too.

Jerry Spinelli

Astounding Science!

★ How small is an atom? If atoms had been falling onto a dish one at a time every second since the earth began, today they would add up only to a speck you could barely see.

★ If you split a photon (a particle of light), making twins out of it, and send each of those twins to opposite ends of the universe, they somehow remain "in touch" with each other. If you impact one, the other (billions of light-years away) reacts.

★ Atoms, the tiny particles that make up everything, are mostly empty space.

★ Light travels so fast it can circle the earth fifty-two times before you come to the end of this sentence.

★ On a clear, moonless night, get out of the city away from lights, and look up. See the band of stars streaming across the sky (you might think they're clouds)? That's the Milky Way. Your galaxy. Your cosmic neighborhood.

An Interview with Jerry Spinelli

Were you a science geek?

Not in my school days. My favorite subject was geography. I became more interested in science when I got out of school and began to read about it on my own. I practically got dizzy over the wonders of the world I live in. Black holes that swallow light . . . quasars brighter than a hundred billion suns . . . particles in two places at once. . . . C'mon, how could you *not* get geeky?

Were you like Will?

In a lot of ways, no. I didn't have a little sister (but I did have a little brother, and yes, he could be pesty). I wasn't interested in astronomy in those days. I didn't play chess. But I was very organized. I kept records of every little thing I did in my Biddy Basketball games. I was very neat. I planned things out. I overthought.

Did you make up that stuff about a proton dying?

No—and yes. In mine shafts deep in the earth—including one in Yellowknife, Northwest Territories, Canada—scientists are trying to catch a proton ceasing to exist. The part I made up is the discovery itself—it hasn't actually happened. Yet.

Are there really star parties?

Sure. They're cool. Eileen and I first attended one at Valley Forge, Pennsylvania. We drove onto a big field and cut our headlights. People were walking around with red caps over their flashlights to keep the light pollution down, so we could see the stars better. Then we just strolled around looking through peoples' telescopes. Some were just little things, even binoculars; others were as big as bathtubs. What a thrill it was when I stood on a little stepladder and looked into an eyepiece and there was Saturn with its rings! I'd seen a thousand pictures, but they all seemed fake and unreal compared to this.

What is the main message of *Smiles to Go*?

Good question. There are a number of messages tucked into the story, but I guess the prime message points to the prime character, Will Tuppence. Think about it. Will is a kid without a Now. He lives in the Future. He's got it all figured out, including a twelve-step master plan that starts with "born" and ends with "Heaven." All neat and tidy and everlasting. Problem is, everybody else is living Now. And Now is messy.

And a new discovery (the aforementioned dying proton) suggests that even Forever won't last, well, forever. Then Will makes discoveries of his own in the persons of his Monopoly-and-pizza partners and his little sister, aka the Pest—and in the end makes the best discovery of all, that Now is where it's at. And it sends the reader a message: Live your life. Love your life. Now. Every second of it. Wring it like a sponge. Forever will take care of itself.

Why are there so many tombstone epitaphs in the story?

It just seemed to fit with the Now vs Eternity scope of the story. An epitaph is literally written in stone, the last word. It's a handy way to condense and sharpen the view of a person—in this case, Will's view of himself.

Are you an expert on the skateboard?

I've never been on one.

I hear Will catches BT kissing Mi-Su. Does this mean Will gets shut out?

Read the book.

The Edge of the Sofa

In the chapter called PD77 Will visits the home of his pal BT. Quoting Will: "When you open his front door you don't see a living room—you see a dump." BT—sloppy, disorganized, impulsive—is the opposite of Will. BT's house reflects this.

I knew such a kid. When I was fourteen, he was the best pitcher on our Pennsylvania state championship Connie Mack Knee-Hi baseball team. He was happy-go-lucky. A leaf in the wind. I learned not to make plans to meet him somewhere, because half the time he wouldn't show up. And when he did, he was late. A phrase from a Kurt Vonnegut novel comes to mind: "He was unstuck in time." If he cared about it (baseball, reading Russian novels), he did it; if he didn't care about it (getting to school on time, homework, studying), he didn't do it. He inspired the character I call BT.

And the house he lived in inspired BT's house. I remember visiting him once. As soon as I opened the front door I knew I was in for something I had never seen before. Newspapers and magazines were stacked from floor to ceiling in the living room and dining room, not to mention all other manner of junk. To get from one spot to another was like navigating

through canyons. A quick glimpse into the kitchen told me I did *not* want to go in there.

I took a seat on the living room sofa. After a minute or so I began to catch movement out of the corners of my eyes. (Your side vision sees movement better than your straight-on vision.) I looked around. Roaches. The place was crawling with roaches. They were on the sofa, the floor, the walls, the newspaper mountains. But that wasn't my only problem. I didn't want to embarrass my friend by letting him know that I knew his house was crawling with bugs. Or to put it another way: I was too chicken to be honest and go screaming the heck outta there.

So I slid my butt up to the tippy-tippy edge of the sofa and sat there until a respectable amount of time had passed and I could say I had to head home for dinner. I ran all the way, pulling my pockets inside-out, scratching my head and shaking my arms to dislodge any unwelcome critters. As I recall, I didn't sleep very well that night.